with
Closed Eyes

Kandise Carlisle

Pink Kiss Publishing Company
Gautier, Mississippi

This book is a work of fiction. Names, characters, places, and incidents either are products of the author's imagination or are used fictitiously. Any resemblance to actual event or locales or persons, living or dead, is entirely coincidental.

Cover designed by CreationsbyDonna@gmail.com

Layout and Interior Designed by:

glendawallace@pinkkisspublishing.com

ISBN 978-0-9851909-8-9

Library of Congress Control Number: 2012909934

Published by: Pink Kiss Publishing Company

P.O. Box 744

Gautier, Mississippi 39553

(228) 366-6828

www.pinkkisspublishing.com

This Book is dedicated to five strong women that I admired and look up to. My mother Goldie Wright, my grandmother Mary Gilchrist, I know you are in heaven smiling down on me thanks for the hard love you showed to me. My aunt Essie James, I love you, I know you are taking care of your mother in Heaven. To my sister Belinda Wells, (RIP). To a special lady that has become a part of my life and has always told me to never give up, Albertine Clifton. To My father Helbert Wells and my step-father Willie Wright, I love you (RIP) George Dickerson my favorite brother in law. And Frederick Thompson, (RIP) nephew it's almost a year but you are missed every day by us. I love you.

Acknowledgments

First of all I want to Thank God for his unconditional love that he has for me. I want to thank you God for placing this gift inside of me and allowing me to share it with the world. God, I love you for you never gave up on me when I was about to throw in the towel. I would always hear the song "Trust Me" that alone let me know that you were carrying me. I want to thank my precious mother for giving me life. Mudear, I love you more than you will ever know. As a child I watched how strong you were and that alone has taught me how to be a Strong Woman. To my beautiful daughters Kaneisha, and Kimuel always follow your dreams and put God first in everything you do and you will never go wrong, I love you. Kendra you are not just a (step-daughter) but a daughter to me I watched you grow into a mother and wife and you have done an excellent job. I love you as if you were my own. To my sister's Sondra and Beverly we have had our up's and down's and yes, you have made me mad as hell but it did not change my love for you. To my sister Brenda, thanks for always checking in on me and when I call you, you are there for me. I love you guys. To my nieces Kenyetta, Jamella, Gabrielle, Danielle, Jackie, Nicole, Yolanda and Daphne, know that I love you and enjoy my family time with you. Jamella, Gabrielle and Danielle you can really work your aunt's nerves but that's ok, lol…Nicole, we know we have our share of conversation on the phone but we are going to make it (inside story), lol...To my Brother Sam and Elbert, I love you guys because you guys know you have a sister's back; all I have to do is call. To my nephews Anthony, Arthur and Anthony thanks for being there for you aunt love you. To the crew Cetonia, Cedric, Annette, Love, Tracy, Marcy, Q, David, Audrey, Derrick, Kim, Terri and Stephanie thanks for letting me write when we are on our trips before I come in on the party. I can say we know how to have a ball, I love you guys. To Davetta, thank you for all your support that you have given me through the years. All I have to do is call you and you step up even with the Red Velvet Cakes lol…To Terri, Angie and Kelvin, thank you for your support in my dream.

To my two favorite cousins from Ohio Marie and Monique, thanks for listening to me read this story before it got this far, I love you both. Keith Ink Heart, God knew what he was doing when he placed you in my life. You told me to take my story and go with it and that's what I did. You are a blessing from God. To Pastor and Minister White, I love you. I'm glad to be in a church where the word comes forth. You said this was the year of Favor and this is Favor for me. To Uncle Butch you would tell me every Sunday don't stop writing, well, look at me now. Thanks for believing in me. Round table ladies: Diane, Katrina and Charlotte, thanks for your support. Glenda, Lord knows I thank you for letting me be a part of this great family of PKP Authors. You took my story and brought it to life, you just don't know how much I appreciate what you have done. I truly love you. To those I may have forgotten charge it to my head and not my Heart. I finally made it. This is the first but not the last. PKP ROCK STARS!!!! Thank You Lord.

Prologue

As Sharon sat at her computer checking her e-mails, feeling tired she knew it was time to tell Darryl that she was expecting, but she did not know how he was going to react to the situation. Sharon had been seeing Darryl for over a year now and he had promised that he would marry her, but every time she brought the subject up he would change it to something else. She could not put her finger on it, but she was beginning to get frustrated with the situation.

Darryl was an incredibly good-looking man. He stood about six-four and weighed about two hundred fifty pounds, with dark skin and a bald head. His lips were so well-defined they looked as if they were drawn on his face. He worked out at the gym every day so that he could stay in shape. He was so good looking he could easily be someone that would grace the cover of a magazine. Women loved him, and always threw themselves at him.

One night when Darryl was at Sharon's house the impossible happened, he left his cell phone! This was unusual because he usually keep his cell phone in his car so he wouldn't be disturbed while he was with Sharon; at least, that is what he told her. But that night, in Darryl's haste to take a shower, he did not realize his phone was still in his pants pocket.

While Darryl was in the shower, his phone rang. Sharon let it go to voice mail and after the message was left, she quietly went to check it. Sharon was shocked to learn that he was married. His wife, Tameka, had left a message saying she had just made it home and would be ready and waiting on him to get off to give him some good loving.

Sharon/Darryl

Darryl was in the shower when Sharon burst in screaming at the top of her lungs about what she had just heard on his cell phone.

"Darryl, you dog! You have been 'round here sleeping with me for over a year now and every time I talk to you about getting married, you want to change the subject. But now it all makes sense, since your *wife* just called to tell you she'd be at home waiting on you!" Sharon screamed as she rolled her neck and sucked her teeth. She could not understand what was going on and why Darryl would lie to her. "Why Darryl? Why did you have to lie to me? You could have told me the truth and let me make that decision on my own."

Darryl immediately became defensive. "What the hell are you doing answer my phone anyway? You do not have the right to do that," he said, grabbing a towel from the rack and wrapping it around his waist before he stepped out of the shower. He was trying to think of how to smooth things over with Sharon.

"No, I didn't, but you are in my house and I can check whatever the hell I want when it's in my house," Sharon retorted back with anger flashing in her eyes. "You forgot this time to leave it in the car and now your secret is out. Now I know why you would never bring it in the house. But I was so blinded by love that I could not see the truth right in front of me," she continued shaking her head. "My mother always told me 'when you lay down with dogs you end up with fleas' and not only have I ended up with fleas, but I have ended up *pregnant* by a flea."

"Hell, no! You are not about to have a baby, so you know what you have to do." Darryl stormed into the bedroom and started getting dressed.

"And what is that Darryl?" Sharon asked as she followed him out of the bathroom.

"You are going to get rid of that situation and not bring trouble to my home."

"Your home? Right about now I don't care anything about you *or* your home. I cannot believe that you have lied to me for over a year. Do you really think I'm going to let this go that easy? Oh no, baby. You fucked with the wrong one. I will not take this with a grain-of-salt. Get your clothes and get the hell out of my house! And don't you ever call or come by here or my job, because I promise you I will have you arrested. The only thing I will let you know about is when I have this baby. I will let you know if it's a girl or boy. Oh, and one more thing Darryl, do not underestimate me about this baby, I might just change my mind and get in contact with you. GOOD BYE!"

As Darryl began to gather all of his belonging and put them in a duffle bag he thought about how careless he had become. He really did love Sharon; she was everything he didn't have at home. She was not controlling like his wife Tameka, telling him to do this and to do that like she was his mother instead of his wife. As much as

Darryl hated to admit it, he did not want to leave Sharon, but he knew she was upset with him and would not hear a word he had to say at that particular moment. So he did what he was asked to do, he got his stuff and left.

As Sharon watched Darryl out of her living room window, tears silently rolled down her face. She was so distressed by the situation that she stood in the same spot for over an hour. By the time she laid down it was almost midnight. Sharon just could not get the "episode" out of her mind, let alone eat anything. She put in one of her favorite movies, *How Stella Got Her Groove Back,* and watched it until she doze off to sleep. By 3:00 a.m. the ringing of her phone woke her from her sleep. Looking at the caller ID she saw that it was Darryl. Sharon did not answer the phone because she didn't want to deal with him. He knew that Wednesday's were her early mornings to go in to work, so why would he even think about calling her at this time of the morning? The red light flashed indicating he had left a message. *I refuse to deal with his foolishness right now. I'll check it in the morning,* she thought as she turned over and went back to sleep.

It seemed only minutes later when the alarm on her nightstand sounded. Still half asleep, Sharon dragged herself out of bed. She went into the bathroom to take a hot shower and try to wash away the scene from last night. Sharon stepped into the shower and let the hot water cascade down her back. It felt good, and she stood there for the longest time just letting the water hit every inch of her body. Finally, she emerged from the shower and began to lather her body with the apple scented lotion that she loves so much. Darryl had given it to her as a birthday gift two months ago. After she finished putting on her lotion, she stepped into her closet and picked out a beige Versace pants suit, put on her diamond hoop earrings, and pulled her locks up in a ponytail. After applying her makeup Sharon took a final look in the mirror—it was flawless. She grabbed her bag and headed out the door to work. She got into her blue Range Rover, pulled out of her driveway and headed towards the freeway. Sharon was glad that it was Wednesday, because the early morning traffic would not be heavy. Once on the freeway, she put in her CD and headed north listening to the smooth voice of Sade.

Tameka

"Hey baby, what's wrong, you look upset? Did something happen at work?" Tameka asked as Darryl walked through the door.

"No, just tired, and need to get some sleep," Darryl replied as he walked past her, not bothering to even glance at her.

Tameka was a short light-skinned woman. She had dark hair that she kept cut short and her makeup was always worn to perfection. She and Darryl had been married for ten years, but a couple of years ago things seemed to become distant between the two. Tameka knew that something was wrong with Darryl, she knew his ins-and-outs, she even knew that he had being sleeping around with someone, but did not know who.

"Darryl, do you want something to eat before you go to sleep?" Tameka asked, still trying to connect with her husband.

"Nah, I'm fine."

As Tameka put dinner away she knew that something was bothering Darryl. She was willing to bet it had something to do with his affair. Although she had no clue *who* he was involved with, she promised herself that she would make it her business to find out. She was getting sick and tired of Darryl coming home with these different attitudes all of the time. It was about time that she let him in on what she knew.

"Darryl we need to talk," Tameka began.

"I don't feel like talking right now, I just want to go to sleep," he said releasing a deep sigh.

"Well, I want to talk and I want to discuss your behavior."

"*My* behavior? Woman what are you talking about? You need to get out of my ear with this mess," he continued mumbling to himself.

"I'm talking about the affair you are having!" Tameka said folding her arms across her chest, preparing for him to deny it. "Do you think that I'm crazy? Women know these things and I have been married to you long enough to know when something is not right. I also know that this is not something that has just started. This has been going on for a while now, and I have been patient long enough," she said getting angrier as she continued, "not saying anything, keeping this to myself, trying to keep up a good front that our marriage is solid. But I'm sick and tired of it. This shit has gone too far and you need to figure out what you are going to do about it." Tameka slapped her hand on her hip and stared at Darryl waiting for an answer.

"I'm not going to take this any longer. I don't know what you're talking about, so I'm going to do just what I said and that is, go to sleep."

"No the hell you're not! We are going to continue this discussion tonight. I have put this off long enough."

"I don't give a damn what you say, you are not going to make me admit to something and talk about something that I do not know anything about."

"So, what you are telling me is that I'm imaging things?" she questioned with a raised eyebrow.

"Exactly!"

By this time, Darryl walked out of the den where he was sitting watching TV, grabbed his keys and walked out the front door.

"Where the hell are you going at this time of the morning?" Tameka asked.

Without answering, Darryl kept walking to his car. He slammed the door to his car and peeled out of the driveway. Darryl had driven about forty-five minutes before he stopped to call Sharon to apologize for the pain he had caused her. Darryl really loved Sharon in a special way and he did not want to lose her, but at the same time, he knew that he had a wife at home who really loved him. But there was no denying that his feelings for Tameka had vanished a long time ago. She was too controlling and always demanding things. He was sick of it and wanted out. Darryl knew he planned on leaving his wife at some point, but he just didn't know when. He wanted a life with Sharon, someone who really understood him and did not just want him for his money. He took a chance and called Sharon to explain everything. He knew she would be sleep, but he decided to call her anyway.

He reached over to the passenger seat to get his phone before dialing her number. It went to voicemail.

"Hey Sharon, I know it's early, and you have to get up for work, but I just wanted to let you know that I'm so sorry. I should have told you from the beginning that I was married and let you decide if you wanted a relationship with me or not. My wife knows I have being seeing someone, but she doesn't know who. She told me this tonight, I know that this..." The phone beeped to let Darryl know that he ran over. Darryl redialed her number again and listened to Sharon's voice message. He continued where he left off. "I know that this does not change anything, but Sharon I really love you. I want a life with you. I have messed up tremendously and all I ask of you is to let me explain everything. Please? Could I have a moment with you just to talk about what I did and didn't do? I also want to apologize for what I said to you tonight about getting rid of the baby. I did not mean that, I was just upset at the time and said some things that were totally out of character of me.

By the time Darryl got through leaving Sharon that message, his phone started ringing. When he looked at the caller ID it said *HOME.*

"Yeah!" he barked into the phone.

"Are you coming back home, or are you going to stay out tonight?"

"Look, Tameka, I'm not in the mood for a confrontation, I need to get some rest for in the morning. I will be back home, but I'll be sleeping in the guest room so I can get some rest.

"Okay," she replied softly.

Tameka knew all she had to do was put some good loving on him when he got back, and as usual, he would be under her spell. She did not know how long it was going to take her to get her man back to the way they used to be, but she was not giving up without a fight. Tameka lay in bed waiting on her husband and thinking about how she was going to seduce him once he got home. She had taken a shower and put on her black lace negligee, sprayed on her favorite perfume and gave her reflection in the mirror a seductive smiled once she was finished.

She heard the garage door go up and down, she turned on her side like she was asleep because she knew that he would check on her before he went into the guest room.

Darryl walked in their room and got his pj's. By the time he reached the door he heard her voice.

"Hey baby, I'm sorry about tonight. I shouldn't have said anything to you about that. Can you forgive me?" Tameka asked as she turned over to face him.

"Yea, but all I want to do right now is to take a shower and go to bed. It's late and I have to get up in the morning," he sighed.

"Well, can I have a kiss from you before you do that?" Tameka asked seductively, as she got out of bed and stood in front of the door blocking his exit.

"Look Tameka, I know you just like you know me, and you're trying to get me to come to bed with you, but like I told you, I'm going to bed in the guest room."

"Darryl, please, just one kiss. You are still my husband or have you forgotten that?"

"No, I have not."

"Then what is your fucking problem?" Tameka spat no longer able to contain her anger.

"See, this is why I didn't want to come back home. I knew we would get back into it. Will you just leave me alone and let me get into the shower?"

"Sure I will, but not until you give me what I asked for."

Darryl turned around and gave Tameka the kiss that she so longed for. As he kissed her, she grabbed his dick and stroked it up and down. Darryl could not let the moment get him weak, so he pushed Tameka away from him. An angry frown spread across her face.

"You know you want me, so why are you fighting this?" Tameka asked teasingly.

"Tameka, leave me alone," Darryl replied as she followed him into the guest bedroom. Darryl began undressing before heading into the bathroom with Tameka hot on his heels.

"What the fuck is wrong with you? Are you seriously going to deny all this?" she gestured at her lingerie clad body.

Darryl just shook his head in dismay and stepped into the shower.

Tameka stormed out of the bathroom and into the room where Darryl had left his pants on the floor. She begin to search for his cell phone because she was going to find out who this woman was that had her husband so turned out. She scrolled down until she saw an unfamiliar number. Tameka wrote the number down and knew she would be giving this person a call tomorrow to find out what was going on.

Sharon

Sharon got out of her car and walk into the building where she works. As she got on the elevators to proceed to the eighth floor, she had a flashback of last night. She had forgotten to listen to her answering machine before she left but what she really wanted was to have a good day before she listened to anything Darryl had to say. As the elevator doors opened and before she stepped off, she felt her cell phone vibrate, Sharon pulled her phone out of her bag and without looking at the number on the caller ID she answer it.

"Hello."

"Yes, I really don't know whom I'm speaking with but I got your number out of my husband's phone. First of all, my name is Tameka, and Darryl is my husband. I know you have been seeing him. I told him last night that I have let this little charade go on long enough, and I'm tired. I think it is very low of you to sleep with another woman's husband. You are a nasty *bitch* and I hate you for this. I really don't care if you let him know that I called, because like I said before, I told him this last night. I will not give up on him easily and if you think this is going to keep on going between you two, you are sadly mistaken. I will fight to the end before I let some bitch like you come in and ruin our family," Tameka hissed.

After getting over the initial shock, Sharon finally spoke. "You listen here Tameka. First of all, I didn't know that Darryl was married, I just found out last night when you called him. You see, Darryl has never before brought his phone into my house, and last night he forgot. That is how I found out about your ass, and when I did I put him out of my house and told him not to ever come back. Now, I'm telling you don't ever call my phone again, if you know what's good for you! You really don't want to go there with me. I'm really trying to spare your feelings on some things, so the next time you call me you are going to wish that you hadn't," Sharon said and hung up before Tameka could reply.

By the time Sharon sat down and calmed her nerves, she didn't know whether to call Darryl or her girlfriend Monica. Her phone rang and brought her out of her trance.

"Mrs. Davis, your first appointment is here."

"Okay. Give me five minutes and send her in. By the time Sharon came out of her bathroom her first appointment was coming into her office.

"Hi Benita, how are you today?" Sharon greeted her client.

"I'm okay, just been having a hard time trying to focus on the positive and keep the situation of my marriage out of my mind. I know you told me not to think about all of the negative things that went on in my marriage, but I can't help but want to kill that man."

"I know how you must feel, but you have to stop putting all of your energy into this. I know there has to be something that you enjoy doing to take your mind off of things."

"Yes, but it's hard not to think about all this man has done to me..." Benita trailed off with a faraway look in her eyes.

"If you allow this situation to keep eating away at you then maybe you need to take my advice and bring your ex with you to your next appointment."

"I don't think that would be a good idea. At some point, you might have to be a witness."

As Sharon continued with her session, she started to feel a little better. Sometimes her work helped her to take her mind off her own problems. By the time she finished with Benita it was almost lunchtime.

"Kimberly, could you please hold my calls if anyone calls for me? I'm about to be on an important call and I don't want to be disturbed."

"Yes, Mrs. Davis."

Sharon dialed her girlfriend Monica's number. The phone rang about four times before she finally answered.

"Hey girl, I was just about to hang up the phone. I assumed you were gone."

"I'm sorry, Shay. Girl, I was in there trying to keep up with this woman on this exercise video," she laughed.

"Why do you do that to yourself? You are fine the way you are and you still go around buying those damn videos trying to make yourself look better than you already do."

"Okay, what is it? I know something is wrong with you when you start cussing because that is not like you. That's *my* department."

"There's nothing wrong. Want to do lunch?"

"Okay, you really need to stop lying. It is around lunchtime, but it's not our scheduled day for lunch, *and* you are cussing. It's Darryl, isn't it? What has he done this time? Is he still beating around the bush about marrying you?"

"No, that can't be it because he's already married."

"What the fuck did you just say? He is already married? To whom, when, and how did you find this out?" Monica continued, not bothering to take a breath between questions.

"Well, you know how he always leaves his cell phone in the car, remember me telling you this when we first start talking?"

"Yes, and please tell me you did not go in his car and go through his phone."

"No!"

"Then what happened?"

"Look, meet me at Applebee's and we will continue this conversation. I'm about to get off, I cannot get anything done today so I'm about to leave. I just finished my appointment for today and I don't feel like messing with any paperwork."

"Okay, give me about forty-five minutes and I'm on my way. This shit here is going to be good. See you in forty-five minutes."

Before Sharon got her stuff together to prepare to leave for the day, she remembered she still had not made the call to Darryl. *Let me get this stuff together before I call him,* she thought. Once Sharon had gotten everything together she sat down to call Darryl.

"Hello."

"Hi Darryl."

"Sharon?"

"Yes, it's me."

"Let me explain to yo—"

Sharon cut him off. "No need to, your wife called and explained everything."

"Say what?!"

"Yes, she called me this morning as I was getting off of the elevator. She said that she talked with you last night about everything."

"She did, and I left you a message to try to explain that she confronted me and said she knew I was having an affair."

"Darryl, how could you?"

"Sharon, I'm really sorry. I did not mean to hurt you like this. I really didn't know how to tell you because I didn't want to lose you. I'm in love with you. I love the way you sleep, the way you look at me when I'm talking about work, and the way you smile when you are cooking and listening to our song that we dance to."

"If you cared anything for me you would have told me the truth from the beginning and I could have made that decision on my own."

"I know, and I'm hurting because of how I have hurt you. I'm not happy at home. You make me happy, that's why I spend so much time with you."

"No, Darryl, you do not love me. What you thought was that I was never going to find out. That was your plan. You don't give a damn about me or this baby that I'm carrying. And by the way, I told your wife not to call me anymore because I will not hesitate to give her something she does not want to know about."

"I don't care if you tell her because I'm leaving her anyway. I'm sick and tired of her, plus, I don't love her."

"You need to think about what you are about to do."

"Look, it's not like we have kids because we don't, this baby that you are carrying will be my first. She can't have kids."

"Darryl, do you really think I would take you back? This same shit you have done to her, you would do it to me. I'm no fool—well, I was for over a year being with you, and all the while your ass was married!"

"Sharon, please don't do this, will you please give me another chance? I need you, you make me happy."

"I'm sorry, but you have made your bed so you are going to have to lie in it."

"I will not give up so don't think for once that I am. We are going to be together."

"Darryl, I have to go. I'm running late."

As Sharon hung up the phone she knew she was still in love with Darryl. *It's going to be hard moving on without him,* she thought. Her heart was telling her to stay with him and work this thing out, but her mind was saying otherwise. Sharon missed the way he touched her and the thought of it made her rub her stomach. She looked at the time. She had only ten minutes to get to Applebee's. She called Monica on her way out of the office to let her know she was running late.

Monica

"Hey girl, where are you? I got here much sooner than I expected," Monica said.

"I'm on my way. I ended up talking on the phone to Darryl and I lost track of time."

"So what did he say?"

"I will let you know everything once I get there."

Monica was a dark-skinned girl with jet black hair. She kept her hair cut short and she liked to wear tight clothes. When she was growing up, she would wait until her mom's company came over, and she would go and find something tight to put on; from tight shirts to the pants and she would prance around for the boys outside while her mom was entertaining her company.

Once Sharon and her family moved in down the street and she started high school with Monica, she took notice of how Sharon dressed. She began to notice that even though Sharon dressed somewhat conservative she would still get the attention of the boys. One day, Monica asked Sharon to help her to start dressing like that, and from then on, they have been the best of friends.

Monica wore a size six, she was about 5'4 and she loved to wear her stilettos. She had the most beautiful green eyes. Growing up, people always asked her how did she get green eyes and have a black mother. She would tell them to ask her mom. Even now when she was asked about her eyes, she gave the same answer. While Monica waited on Sharon she sat and talked to her brother on her cell phone about her mom. Monica's mom had been sick for a couple of years now. She would go and visit her once in a while, but after she left Atlanta and went to UAB in Birmingham, it was very seldom that she went home to visit. She was not close to her mom like her brother was.

Sharon/Monica

When Sharon made it to the restaurant she found Monica seated in a booth in the corner. "Hi girl, I'm sorry that I'm late," she said as she took a seat across from her friend.

"It's okay. I've being talking with my brother until you got here," Monica replied looking anxiously at her friend.

"How is he doing?"

"You know, he's doing well. His job is going well for him."

"I bet it is, being a big time lawyer and all. How is your mom?" Sharon asked scanning the menu.

"She's doing as best as she can. He's trying his best not to put her in a nursing home. Right now, someone comes to the house and looks after her when he's out."

"Now that's a real man. When you can find one who will take care of his mother the way your brother does, then you've found a *real* man."

"Yeah, he is a good man. Soooo, what's going on with you?"

"Girl, you will not believe what has happened."

"Okay. I know that Darryl has a wife and you went through his phone."

"Look Monica, I did not just sit down and go through his phone. You know how I told you he loves to leave his phone in the car when he is over? Well, this time as he was rushing into the house to take a shower, he forgot and left his phone in his pocket. It rang, but I didn't answer it. When it beeped to let him know he had a voice mail, I listened to the message. That's when I found out he has a wife. She left him a message telling him she had just gotten home and would be waiting on him to make love," Sharon said rolling her eyes.

"Oh no she did not!"

"Girl, lower your voice, you have people staring at us."

"What did you do after the message?"

"Burst in the bathroom and went off, told him to get his stuff and get out of my house."

"I know you went back to our young days," Monica chuckled as she remembered how feisty her friend could be when she was pissed about anything.

"Monica, I can't really say what I wanted to do, I was so hurt, and I still am. I really do love him and to top it off, I'm having his baby."

"*WHAT?* Sharon, please tell me that you are kidding. What are you going to do with a baby? You have a career that keeps you moving most of the time."

"I know, but I just cannot abort this baby. That wouldn't be right. God would not be pleased with that."

God is not pleased with you sleeping with a married man either," Monica retorted rolling her eyes and taking a sip from her drink.

"How the hell was I supposed to know he was married? I just found that shit out last night."

"I'm sorry, Shay. I didn't mean that, please forgive me. Shay you are my best friend, we have been through a lot together from high school to college and I'm not the one to talk because I've had my share of shit. I'm going to be there for you regardless of what you decide. I got your back."

"Thank you, Monica."

"Girl, please! You are my girl and I love you."

"I love you too."

The girls ordered their food, ate and talked about work and life. It had been a while since they'd had a day like this one. They talked and laughed and shared some other things together.

"Sharon, I cannot believe that she had the nerve to call and tell you something like that. I didn't think women still did that kind of mess."

"I just wish that he would have told me and let me make that decision on my own instead of me finding out like this. I'm just tired of black men being so damn stupid."

"Girl, I know what you mean. Time you think you have found the right one, some shit jumps out of the bag."

After about two hours of talking and laughing the girls decided to see one another on their regular lunch day.

"Call me and let me know that you made it home safely."

"I will, Monica. And you be careful."

Sharon

As Sharon drove home she listened to one of her gospel CD's by Richard Smallwood, "I'll Trust You." As she drove, she hummed along to the music and rocked from side to side. She had been brought up in the church, but now that she was grown, she would go every now and then. Her mother had always told her to never put God last, always put him first no matter how bad the situation may be. She knew she needed to get back in the church and now was the time. As she continued to drive and listen to the song she began to feel more relaxed about everything.

Sharon pulled up into her driveway and by the time she got out of the truck she was tired. All she wanted to do was get in the house, call her girlfriend, and go to sleep. Even though her day had not been long hours, it just felt long because of all the mess she had gone through in the past twenty-four hours. Sharon just wanted this day to be over with. She walked into her home, kicked off her shoes, and picked up the phone to call her friend. "Hey Monica, just wanted to let you know that I made it home and everything is okay." Once she left the message with Monica she took off all her clothes and turned on the shower. Sharon was so relieved and the hot water running over her naked body helped to calm her down. She was thankful that she had a friend like Monica that she could count on when she needed her the most.

As Sharon was getting out of the shower she heard her phone ringing.

"Hello."

"Hey girl, I just wanted to let you know that I got your message."

"Okay, good. Well, I'm about to go in here and fix me some hot milk and read a book. I'm hoping it will relax me and I can get some sleep."

"Do you need me to come over later and stay the night, just in case that fool tries to come by or call again?"

"Girl, no! Darryl was warned not to come this way. I told him if he did, I would call the police."

"You are crazy," Monica laughed.

"Yes, I am crazy in love with a jackass," Sharon responded with a laugh.

"Girl, shut up, you got me over here about to pee on myself laughing at your crazy butt. Well, what are you going to do about the baby? Have you given that any thought?"

"Yes, I have and I'm going to have this baby. There is no way that I can get an abortion, God will provide, He always does," Sharon replied, remembering her mother's words.

"Well, girlfriend, you are right about that. He always does, and even though I know I don't go to church like I should, I still do pray every day and every night."

"I'm glad you and I both do."

Darryl/Tameka

"Look woman, I'm not about to keep arguing with you about this. All you've ever wanted was to treat me like a child instead of your husband. You are not my mother so stop acting as if you are."

"What the hell do you mean I act like your mom?"

Darryl was looking at Tameka with so much fury in his eyes that they looked like they were about to pop out of his head. "You do. You like to give me orders all of the time—do this, and do that. I get tired of that shit." At this moment Tameka could not believe what she was hearing coming out of her husband's mouth. "You know what Tameka? I'm sick and tired of this, so I'm going to let you in on something you are not going to like. For the past year I have being sleeping with the woman I love. Her name is Sharon, and the reason I turned to her in the first place is because of what I just told you. You act more like my mom than my wife. I've tried to let you know this on many occasions, but you wouldn't listen. You were always brushing me off. So, one day we got into an argument and I went out walking in the mall. That's when I met Sharon," he continued, relieved to finally be getting this off his chest. "Unlike you, she knows how to listen without always running her mouth. She hardly complains, and she knows how to cook. She didn't have a clue that I was married because I didn't tell her. I wasn't sure she would be able to take it, but after all that has happened in the last twenty-four hours, I think back and wish I would have told her. I wish I had let her make the choice whether or not she wanted to be with me. I never wanted her to find out the way she did. Yes, I love her and always will. It's you that I don't love anymore and as of tonight, I will not continue living in this house with you until I decide what I'm going to do."

Tameka was looking at Darryl like he had lost his mind. *How dare he speak to me as if I am nothing! After all the shit he has put me through,* she thought to herself. Tameka had so much fire in her eyes if looks could kill, Darryl would be a dead man. She couldn't contain her anger any longer. Without being aware of it, she had balled up her fist, and her body was shaking. The next thing that Darryl saw was her charging at him.

"What the hell did you just say?" Tameka asked as she began swinging on Darryl. She had caught him off guard so right now she had the advantage of whipping his ass.

Darryl pushed her off him. She was like some kind of wild animal, punching and clawing at him all at the same time. Once he got her off of him he stood over her, to let her know not to try that shit again.

"Look Tameka, don't try that again. I don't want to hit you. All I want to do is leave since it's obvious I won't be getting any sleep tonight. Enough has been said here tonight and hitting one another is not going to solve anything. I just wanted to tell you the truth. I'll admit I was wrong, but you have a right to hear this. Although I was wrong for what I've done, this is how I feel and there is nothing that's going to change it right now. I'm sorry for all of this, but it has to be this way." Darryl began walking toward the kitchen so that he could go out to the garage and get into his car. Tameka threw a vase at him as he walked away, only missing him by inches.

Tameka

"You bastard! After all that I have done for us this is the thanks I get? How could you fall in love with someone else? I'm your wife. I have never tried to treat you like I was your mother. That is what you saw. I may have asked you to do a lot of things, but as a man you should take time out to do what needs to be done for this house and for us without *me* having to tell you," she said with a defeated sigh. "You were always lazy. You never showed any motivation unless it came down to your job. I have always loved you as a husband, not my child. I cannot believe you had the nerve to tell me something like this, but I hope your ass rots in hell. Once you walk out that door, you'd better take all your shit with you. Do not come back this way for anything."The veins in Tameka's neck popped out as she spoke. "If you leave anything, I'll put it on the porch and you can pick it up there. Getting involved with you was the worst mistake I've ever made. My mother warned me about you, but you will reap what you sow," Tameka continued with a disgusted look on her face. "I guess you can go over to *her* house now and live," she stated crossing her arms over her chest.

"No, I can't," Darryl said with his hand on the doorknob before turning to glare at Tameka. "After she found out I was married, she doesn't want to see me anymore," Darryl replied sadly.

This infuriated Tameka even more. *How can he care so much about how she feels but not about my feelings?* Tameka thought. "Well, good for you. Now you don't have either one of us. GET THE HELL OUT OF HERE!" she screamed angrily as Darryl stormed out and slammed the door behind him.

Tameka was so hurt she cried herself to sleep. Shards of broken glass from the vase she had thrown at Darryl lay scattered across the floor. She thought about how she had called Sharon and the manner in which she'd spoken to her, and she knew it was wrong. But she wasn't about to call back to apologize. She wondered what had happened to their marriage and when did it all happen. She knew sometimes she would act possessive about things with Darryl, but she never knew he felt this way. *He could have talked with me about this stuff, instead of keeping it to himself,* she thought to herself. *Was I that bad that he had to go out and meet someone else? If our marriage was that bad we could have talked this out or at least got some help.* Tameka continued to mull over her situation as she drifted off to sleep.

Darryl

I have really messed up. First, I lose the woman of my dreams and then my wife. I should have done the right thing and told Sharon about me. I do not blame her if she does not want to see me ever again. Who would have thought that it would come down to this?

Darryl was sitting at the bar drinking a beer thinking about all that had happened. He was upset about the mess that he had created and he wanted to talk with Sharon. He wanted to see her and tell her how sorry he was for everything, even for asking her to get an abortion. *Man, I got to fix this and the first thing I need to do is get myself together, get a divorce, and get Sharon and my child. I refuse to allow my child to grow up without a father,* Darryl thought as he downed another beer.

Darryl called his friend Marcus to see if he was at home. He wanted to stop by to talk with him about what had happened, plus he needed somewhere to lay his head for the night.

"Hey Man, what's going on?"

"Man, just sitting here looking at TV. What are you up to?" Marcus replied.

I need to come by and talk with you about something, is it okay?"

"Hell yeah, I can used the company. You don't have to stop and get anything to drink, I have plenty of that."

"What about food?"

"I have some leftover pizza."

"Naaah…I'll stop and get us some Krystal."

"Cool, see you soon."

Darryl pulled up in front of Marcus's house about forty-five minutes later with Krystal's."

Marcus greeted him at the door. "Hey, my man, what's up?" he asked, giving him a pound.

Darryl sighed, "Man, if only I could turn back the hands of time, I would," he said handing the fast food bag to Marcus.

"Well, let's go in the den so I can hear all about this."

"Cool, because you are not going to believe your ears," Darryl stated as he followed Marcus into the den and took a seat on the sofa.

"Don't tell me you have done something to Sharon again," Marcus said, picking up the TV remote and turning the volume down.

"Not only to Sharon, but to Tameka too," Darryl replied shaking his head.

What the hell happened, man?"

"Well, you know how I told you that I would leave my phone in the car whenever I'm at Sharon's house?"

"Yeah."

"Well, this time I forgot."

"Don't tell me Sharon went through your phone?"

"No man, but Tameka called and left a message and Sharon listened to it, that's when the shit hit the fan," Darryl admitted shaking his head.

"I hate to say this, but I told you to be up front with the girl because she was the cool type."

"I know, I know, man. I hate that I didn't listen to you but I guess it had to happen this way."

"So what is Tameka saying?"

"We have being arguing like crazy, so I left her. I told her I didn't love her anymore."

"You told Tameka that?" Marcus asked in disbelief.

"Yeah, and got a vase thrown at me, missed me by an inch," Darryl replied holding up his fingers to indicate how close the vase actually got to his head.

"Man, you got some serious shit going on right now and for once I can say that I'm glad it's not me but your ass." Marcus chuckled happy not to be in his friend's shoes.

Both men start laughing at the statement that Marcus made because it was usually Marcus caught up in drama with the many different women that he messed around with.

"Man, is it okay for me to crash over here tonight? I'll go and find a room or something tomorrow on my lunch break."

"You know that is not a problem, we have been friends since we were kids. You are the brother that I never had. You can stay as long as you like man. I'm here for you. I just hope that everything works out for the best," Marcus stated, genuinely concerned about his friend.

"Me too."

"You know that Tameka is not going to take this lightly, right?"

"Oh, don't you think I already know? She called Sharon this morning. The only way she could have gotten the number was to get it from my phone. I have so much going on in my head right now I don't know what to do. On top of everything else, Sharon is going to have my baby!"

"You know Darryl, I'm going to fix me another Jack Daniel's so I can be well prepared for whatever else you might surprise me with." Marcus laughed lightly as he walked over to the bar. "Do you want one?" he asked, raising his glass in the air.

"No thanks, I'm going to get the bags out of the car. I need to get to bed man, I'm tired as hell."

"Well I'm going to have me one more drink and then crash myself. Look Darryl, seriously, I hope you take your time and think everything out logically; make the right decision on things. I got your back and you can stay here as long as you like because I really can use the company. It will be like old times when we were in college."

"Thanks, man. Now I just have to figure out a way to tell my mom what's going on. But I know it won't be tomorrow."

"Well, you better get to her before Tameka does," Marcus warned.

"Damn! You are right about that shit, because her and my moms are very close. She thinks of Tameka as the daughter that she never had, and this is really going to hurt her."

"I know, that's why you gotta get to her and explain what has being going on with the two of you before she does," Marcus replied, taking a long sip of his drink.

"I hear you."

The guys went into separate bedrooms and went to bed. It had been long hours for Darryl and all he wanted was some sleep. As he slept he dreamt about a little girl with long black hair. Her eyes were round and bright and her smile was wide. When Darryl spoke to the little girl that's when Sharon called for her to come. That's when Darryl knew in his heart that she was carrying his daughter. He had to make things right between them.

Darryl

Darryl woke up late for work the next morning, but by it being his company it really didn't matter because he was the boss. Even though he was the boss he still made a good impression to his employees by doing things the same as he would have them to do. So since he was already late he decided to called in to his secretary and inform her that he would not be coming in today.

"Good morning, Barnes Construction Company. How may I help you?"

"Hi Marie, this is Mr. Barnes."

"Good morning, Mr. Barnes. How are you this morning?"

"I'm good. I just wanted to call to let you know that I will not be in the office today."

"Okay, sure. Is everything all right?"

"Yes, I just have some business I need to handle."

"OK, so what do you need for me to do?"

"Let Tommy know that I will not be in and to handle everything for me today. Also, let him know that I will call him later to see how things are going. I will also check back with you today to see how everything is going. I'm looking for a call on a bid with a site from Franklin's, so if they call have them call my cell phone."

"I sure will, Mr. Barnes."

"Okay, well you have a great day and I will see you tomorrow."

Darryl got out of bed, took a shower and prepared to get himself together before he started his day. His mom had taught him how to cook when he was little so it wasn't anything for him to cook for himself. He checked to see what Marcus had in his cabinet and refrigerator then he began to fix some eggs and bacon, made a cup of coffee and checked the paper for apartments that would be suitable for him to live in. Once he finished with everything he left to go and talk with his mother.

Darryl/Essie

Essie lived on the east side of town so coming from Marcus' house it would take Darryl around an hour to get there since he stayed on the outside of town. He listened to his music as he traveled along the road thinking how he would explain this whole mess to his mom. He knew how she felt about Tameka and their relationship so it was going to be hard for him. Darryl's mom was a retired teacher at the high school that he attend as a child and his dad had passed away six years ago, so it was important to Darryl to keep a check on his mother at all times. Even if it was only just calling her every day to make sure that she was okay.

When Darryl pulled his vehicle up to the curb in front of his mother's house she was outside in her yard planting flowers. She looked up and saw him walking up the sidewalk and instantly a big smile came across her face. Essie was seventy-five years old, but she still carried a look of a fifty year old woman. Even though she had wide hips and a big butt she carried it well. It made her look good for her age. Her salt and pepper colored hair hung past her shoulders and her skin was a warm caramel. She had this mole that was planted right above her lip that made her look unique. She was a phlegmatic person so anytime someone came to her about a situation it was common for her not to get excited because she already knew how to handle the situation.

"Hey, baby. How are you today?"

"I'm good," Darryl said giving his mom a warm embrace and a kiss. "And I see you just cannot seem to stay out of this yard," he teased playfully.

"Boy please, you know that I have been doing this all my life. This is my second baby," she replied, rolling her eyes playfully at his comment.

"I know mom. Dad use to tell me 'I don't care what you do son, please do not mess up your mother's yard.' I would ask him why and he would respond by saying, 'if you want to live you need to just leave the yard alone'."

"Well, one thing I can say is that he was right about that. So what are you doing off today? I'm use to seeing you in the evenings, not early mornings," his mother said, eyeing him suspiciously.

"I needed to talk with you about something very important, and I need your advice on some things."

"Okay, let me plant this last flower and I will be inside, but in the meantime, I have some freshly made tea in the refrigerator and those homemade biscuits that you love so much."

"You ain't said nothing but a word, I will see you when you come in," Darryl replied, anxious to get inside to his mom's famous homemade biscuits.

Essie continued to finish up what she was doing. By the time she finished and went back inside, she found Darryl sitting at the kitchen table. He had drunk two glasses of tea and had eaten a couple of biscuit.

"So what's going on with you, what happened?" his mom asked taking a seat at the table across from him getting right to the point. "Son, I know you, you are my child and I can look at your face and tell when things are not right with you. I'm your mother and I'm here for you regardless."

"Thanks, mom, I needed to hear that."

"Okay, then talk to me," she said, looking him straight in the eyes.

Darryl took a deep breath before he began to tell his mother what happened. He knew that she would not get all bent out of shape because she never does. That has always amazed him how his mom could remain cool in certain situations.

Well, what's going on, son?"

"Mom, I have messed up. It started over a year ago. Tameka and I have not been getting along for a while now, and things are not getting any better between us. A lot has gone on, and I'm just really sick of it."

"Darryl, I know. I could tell something wasn't right by the way you have been looking lately when you come by to check on me, but I didn't want to get into your business until you came to me with it. But let me share something with you, you have to do what is right for you and not me or anyone else. I'm not saying that I don't love Tameka because I do, but just because of the way I feel about her doesn't give you a right to stay in something that is making you unhappy.

"Well, I really don't think that you will feel the same when I finish telling you this."

"Go on."

"We got into a big argument about a year ago, I stormed out of the house mad as hell—sorry about the cussing—went to the mall to try and let off some steam, in the meantime, while I was sitting at the table in the food court, I saw this woman walk in and...I don't know, something inside of me just went crazy over her. I had to talk to this woman and find out who she was. So I walked over to her and introduced myself, and asked if I could have a minute of her time. She sat down while she waited on her drink and we began to talk. One thing lead to another, we exchanged numbers and started communicating."

"Does this woman know that you are married?"

"At the time she didn't, she just discovered this news Tuesday night."

"Darryl, no."

"Yes, I kept it from her and when Tameka called and left a message on my cell phone that's how Sharon found out."

"So how are you going to explain this to your wife?"

"She knows."

"What?" his mom asked in disbelief.

"Mom, Tameka knows everything. She told me that she knew I had being sleeping around because of the way I was treating her and how I was acting."

"What are you two going to do? This other woman, what did you say her name was?"

"Sharon."

"What does this Sharon have to say about all of this?"

"Besides being hurt she will not talk to me. She told me that I should have told her the truth and she could have made up her mind from that point."

"You know, she's right. Darryl, you cannot play with a woman's heart like that, it's not right. You knew that you were married and I don't care how bad the circumstances were you just don't do this type of stuff, I did not raise you to be this type of man."

Mom I know, but you just don't know what I've have to go through at home with this woman. It's not easy. It seems like everything I do she has something to say about it. Tameka acts more like my mother than my wife and I have told her this many times."

"So what are you going to do?"

"I don't know right now, but I am staying at Marcus' until I figure it out."

"Say what?"

"I'm staying with Marcus," Darryl repeated again.

"You know if your father was living he would not approve of this mess, but I'm not the one to take sides. I just want you to be happy. This is your life, the only thing I can do as your mother is to give you my advice. It's up to you what you do with it."

"I hear you mom, I appreciate you being honest with me and I hope what I'm about to tell you will not change the way you see me."

"Son, I will never see you any other way but as my son. I may not agree with the decisions that you make, but I'll always love you."

"Thanks mom. What will you say to a grandson or granddaughter?"

"Lord Have Mercy! Out of all this mess you and Tameka are about to have my child? Son, you have to make your marriage right."

Darryl raised his hands for his mom to hold up, knowing what he was getting ready to tell her would probably knock her out of the chair that she was sitting in. "Mom, it is not Tameka who is pregnant, it's Sharon, the woman that I was having an affair with."

"What? Darryl, how could you? Lord Have Mercy, help us."

"Mom, please listen. I know that you are disappointed in me but we did not plan this."

"Well you had to know when you were out there that something like this was bound to come up."

"I did at one point, but I always used protection."

"You should have been at home with your wife instead of in someone else's bed. Oh yes! Your father is turning over in his grave right now," she said, fanning her hand in front of her face like she was hot.

While Darryl and his mom continue to talk, her telephone rang. She looked at the caller ID and to her surprise, it was Tameka calling. "It's your wife," she said to Darryl. "I'm going to answer it but I'm not going to lie for you," she continued, rolling her eyes at her son.

"I already know this, mom."

"Hello."

"Hey Mom Essie, how are you?" Tameka asked.

"Good baby and you?"

"Not so good. I really do need to talk to you. I would go over to my mother's house, but she's out of town. Is it okay for me to come over?"

"Sure, when will you be coming over?"

"I can be there in about thirty minutes. See you soon," Tameka said before hanging up.

"Darryl, Tameka is on her way over. She'll be over in about thirty minutes."

"Mom, I'm really sorry about all of this, but like I said, things have not been good for us in quite some time. But it still didn't give me the right to do what I've done. Not only have I made a mess of Tameka's and my life, but I have also made a mess of Sharon's as well."

"Is she going to keep the baby?"

"Yes. She did say that she would let me know what sex the baby is, but she promised not to cause any problems. She is so mad at me right now, and will not talk with me, but Tameka does not know about this baby right now. Let me just tell you this before I go since she's on her way. Tameka called Sharon and went off on her, I'm just grateful that Sharon didn't say anything. She did say if she called her again she would not hesitate to tell her about the baby."

"Thank God, because that does not need to be told right now," his mom said continuing to fan herself.

"Let me get out of here before she gets here."

"Okay baby, call me tomorrow. I would like to meet this Sharon if she don't mind."

"Mom, she won't even talk to me right now."

"Call me tomorrow and I will get her number from you and talk with her myself."

"Okay."

Tameka/Essie

As Tameka traveled down the highway towards 65 south, she though back on the first day that she met Darryl. She was at a company party and when she looked across the room she looked straight into his eyes. She tried to turn her head, but he saw her and started to smile at her. Tameka smiled back and turned back toward the bar where she was sitting. After a couple of songs played and she'd had a couple of drinks, Tameka got off of her stool to leave when someone tapped her on the shoulder.

"Hi, I'm Darryl."

"Hi Darryl, I'm Tameka," she said accepting his extended hand.

"Leaving already? The night is still young," Darryl replied.

"Yes, I have an early appointment tomorrow."

"On a Saturday?"

"Yes, people can work on Saturday's," Tameka said with a raised eyebrow.

"I'm not saying that but a good looking woman like you shouldn't be working anyone's job on a Saturday.

You should be letting someone take you out on the town and showing you a good time."

"Sorry to disappoint you, but I can do that by myself."

"Well, if you were my woman you would not be working tomorrow, we will be out on the floor dancing the night away."

"Do you do this with all the ladies that you hit on at parties?"

No. I'm very particular about the women I talk too. Let me have one dance before you leave and I promise I will not bother you after the dance."

"Since you promise I will dance with you, but only one dance."

"Okay, sure. You have my word."

One dance turned into four straight dances. Before they left the party they were enjoying each other's company. They exchanged phone numbers and started dating. The rest is history. Tameka and Darryl were living together six months later, and eight months after that they were married.

As she continued to drive, she smiled at the memories of her and her husband's first time meeting. Tameka began to merge off her exit and continued to drive down Madison Avenue. She then turned off onto Meadow Road and rode two blocks, and pulled up to Mom Essie's house. She scuttled to Mom Essie's house before she could open up the door for her.

"Girl, you know you move fast," Mom Essie said as she opened the door and gave her daughter-in-law a strong hug.

"I just really needed to see you," Tameka replied as Mom Essie led her into the family room. Tameka took a seat on the sofa as Mom Essie settled into her favorite leather recliner.

"Tameka, I already know what you want to talk about. I spoke with Darryl today and he told me everything, but that doesn't mean that I don't have to listen to you. You know I love you like a daughter and I want the best for the both of you. I hate this happened, the devil knows he is really doing his job," Mom Essie continued shaking her head. "Just like it says he comes to *steal, kill, and destroy* and you guys are going to have to do some heavy praying if you want your marriage to work. And if it doesn't work, that doesn't mean that I will love you any less."

"I know, but he has told me that he doesn't love me anymore, and that he wants out of the marriage."

"Baby, you have to give him some time. Men say a lot of things and before you know it, you all will be back together."

"It's different with us, there is another woman involved."

"But she didn't know Darryl was married. I'm not trying to defend her, but this is not just her fault. My son started this and if he knew he was going to commit adultery then he should have told this woman the truth. But that's just like a man, they try to be slick but always end up getting caught."

"You are so right." As Tameka began to tell her side of the story to Mom Essie she began to cry.

Mom Essie tried her best to comfort her and let her know that everything would be okay with her, as long as she prayed and put God first. "Look to him for direction, continue to read your Bible and there is where you will find strength and your answers. I love you and I want you to always remember that. No matter what happens with you and my son you will always carry a special place in my heart."

"Thank you, Mom Essie. I really needed to hear that coming from you. I have always loved you like a mother. You have really been an inspiration to me from the first time I met you. When I could not count on my own mother at times, you were right there for me."

"Baby, this is what the good Lord put me on this earth for, to help people. That is why I loved teaching so much. Some of those hard-headed kids would not listen to half of those teachers, but when they came to my class, they were different."

The two ladies continued to talk. Mom Essie went in the kitchen and began to cook some hamburger steaks and rice with gravy. She made some homemade biscuits and Tameka made more tea since Darryl had just about drunk the first jug. They ate, talked, and laughed. By the time Tameka left, it was dark out and she was feeling much better with herself. She thanked Mom Essie and told her she would be calling her to check on her.

"I will be looking to hear from you. Remember what I said, you are special to me and don't forget to pray and ask God for guidance."

"I will," Tameka said before giving Mom Essie a kiss and heading out the door.

Sharon

Oh! I need to hurry up out of here before I miss my first doctor's appointment, Sharon thought to herself. "Kimberly, have I seen everyone for today?"

"Yes."

"Okay, well I'm about to leave for my doctor's appointment, so if everything is taken care of here you can finish up and take the rest of the day off."

"Okay, I will see you on Monday."

"Well, you have a great weekend."

"Thanks, you too."

As Sharon was driving to her doctor's appointment, she listened to the radio 107.7 talk. It's a talk radio station that discusses everyday life situations. Today the topic was "Why Do Married Men Cheat?" One guy's reason was because your wife begins to let herself go once you get married. "She starts to get fat as hell and don't want to keep herself up or keep the house clean. She begins to bitch about unnecessary shit so what we guys tend to do is start hanging out at the bar because we don't want to go home to that bullshit. When you keep hanging out at the bar or clubs and you meet someone who is the opposite of your wife and start to hang out with her, you begin to fall for her, but you've yet to tell her that you are married. And that is why some of us cheat. That's why I did it," the called admitted.

By the time Sharon pulled up in the parking lot of Dr. Fields' office she was hot as hell from this guy's comment, she wanted to call up to the radio station and give him a piece of her mind. Then she thought, *Is this the reason Darryl cheated on his wife?* She got out of the car with the thought still on her mind, but she blew it off until she finished with her appointment. She was going to call Darryl and have a serious talk with him. She wanted to know why he cheated on his wife.

"Good evening, Sharon. How are you today?"

"I'm good, Gloria." Sharon greeted the receptionist with a smile.

"Well, all you have to do is sign in. We have all of your information. Dr. Fields will be calling you back shortly," she said looking up at Sharon over her glasses, returning her smile.

"Thanks, Gloria." Sharon sat in her doctor's office reading a magazine about parenting. She had been coming to Dr. Fields ever since she was eighteen years old and now she was thirty-five and about to have a baby. Sharon was still scared about all of this because she did not know what her father would think of her. She hadn't told her dad that she was about to have a baby. Her mom had been deceased for some time now and Sharon needed her at this very moment to help her through this.

When the nurse opened the door she called out to the waiting room, "Sharon Davis, come with me please."

"Hi Sharon, how are you doing today?"

"I'm good, besides the morning sickness."

"Well, that's normal. You will experience this up to about your third trimester," she said as she led Sharon into an examination room and closed the door.

Sharon took a seat on the vinyl covered chair. "Oh God!"

"Yeah, I remember my first, I was sick all the time. Let me get your weight, blood pressure and get a urine sample from you." After getting all of this from Sharon she returned to the exam room to wait on the doctor.

"Just change into this gown and sit on the bed, the doctor will be right with you," the nurse stated handing Sharon the flimsy gown.

"Thanks, girl." As Sharon sat on the examination table waiting on Dr. Fields, she wondered how she had allowed herself to get in this situation. It was not like she was trying to have a baby. They used protection and she never once tried to trap Darryl with something like this. This was horrible and she was scared.

"Hi Sharon," Dr. Fields greeted as he walked into the room and closed the door. "It's good to see you today."

"Same here, Dr. Fields."

"So how are you feeling?" he asked as he looked over her chart.

"I'm feeling okay. Just having a bit of morning sickness."

Dr. Fields made a few notes on her chart before putting it down and picking up the bulb of the stethoscope and placing it against Sharon's chest. "Let me listen to you first. Take a deep breath for me." He spent a few minutes checking out her breathing. "Good, you sound good. Now I need for you to lie back on the table, put your feet in the stirrups and bring your body forward to the edge of the table." As Dr. Fields examined

Sharon he talked with her letting her know that everything was normal and she was doing well. "Well Sharon, you are fine. You are in your second trimester so I need for you to take it easy. This is your first child and we don't want any problems, so when you get dressed I need you to come to my office and I will give you all the information you need."

"Okay," Sharon replied. After Sharon got dressed she left the examination room and walked down the hall to Dr. Fields' office.

Sharon knocked lightly on the door before entering Dr. Fields' office and taking a seat across from him. She had been in his office plenty of times, but not for anything like this time. "This is what I want you to do Sharon, these are prenatal vitamins and I need you to take them as instructed daily. They are for you and the baby to help keep up your strength. Every woman has to take these supplements when they are expecting. Some women do, and some choose not to, which is not a good idea. Also, try to eat healthy balanced meals and try to eliminate any junk or fried foods, and a little bit of exercise won't hurt. If you like, you can take some of the classes that are offered, but I will give you these pamphlets and let you read them for yourself. They will explain some things to you. I will see you in a couple of weeks, but if you need me just call. Here is your prescription and you can stop by the front desk and they will schedule your next appointment. But everything is going well so far. We are looking to see a baby around the New Year," the doctor finished with an excited smile.

"Oh My God!"

"What's wrong?" Dr. Fields' asked with a look of concern.

"That's when my mom was born."

"Bless her soul, she would have been so proud of you."

"Yes, she would have, no matter what." Sharon left out of Dr. Fields office, made her appointment at the reception desk, and headed out the door. She got in her vehicle and decided to go to the grocery store before she went home. She was craving a homemade taco salad. Her mind went back to Darryl and she decided when she got home she would call him and ask the questions that she needed answers to.

Marcus

As Marcus was driving home from work in his candy apple red F150, he was thinking about his date tonight with a new chick that he'd met when she came to his office. Marcus was a dentist. When he was little he had a thing with teeth. The first thing that he noticed about a person was their mouth. He made sure that he kept his teeth brushed, went to every dentist appointment, and would always ask questions about the different equipment in his dentist's office. So when he went off to college that's what he majored in. He was on the Dean's List all through college. Marcus was light complexioned, stood around 6'5, and weighed right at 205. Marcus was bald headed and had a nice set of lips that were complimented by his startling white teeth. He put you in the mind of Ray Allen and women were crazy over him. That was one of his problems—the ladies. He just couldn't find the right one that he thought was good enough for him. He would always find something wrong once he had been dating them for about six months.

As he traveled down 280 Highway, he listened to Maxwell's CD and though he would call his boy Darryl.

"Hey man, what's up? Did you talk with your mom's?"

"Yeah man, and you know her. She said what was on her mind without being judgmental, but at the same time lets you know how she really feels. When I told her I was staying with you she was furious! But when I told her about the baby, shit, she was shocked."

"I can just imaging seeing her call out, *'Lord Have Mercy'* and all that Jesus stuff," Marcus laughed lightly fanning himself, mocking Mom Essie.

"Yes, she did." Both men started laughing. "Okay, okay, let's leave my mom alone, but you will not believe what she told me."

"What?"

"That she wants to speak with Sharon."

"You got to be kidding?"

"We are talking about my mother."

"Well, yeah. So are you going to let Sharon know?"

"Not right now, but I will. You know she is not talking to me right now so I'm going to let her cool off and then talk with her."

"Cool. Well man, I'm headed home. Got to get ready for this date tonight."

"Cool, I'll talk with you later. See you when you get here."

Marcus really wanted to settle down with a good woman but he just could not fathom why when he would get close to someone, he began to pull away. He had a great relationship with his mom, but he watched how his dad would do his mom every now and then. He was a good provider but it's like he just had to have other women in his life. So Darryl grew up thinking that it was okay to have more than one woman. As he began to pull up in the gas station his cell phone rang. It was Shelia.

"Hi handsome, are you already gone for today?"

"Yeah, just pulling up at the gas station, so I won't have to make any stops on my way to you tonight."

"So I see we are still on, and you have not reneged on me."

"No, I have not. I'm looking forward to seeing you tonight. You just better be ready for what is about to come, because I'm a TIGER," Marcus chuckled as he gave a deep growl.

Shelia laughed. "You are a mess!"

"Okay, but don't say I didn't warn you. I'm really looking forward to tonight," he said again still smiling. "Well, let me go in and get this gas so that I can get home."

"Alright, talk with you when I see you." As Shelia hung up the phone she laughed at the statement that Marcus had made about being a TIGER, she was ready for this man. From the first time she saw him she knew she had to have him, if only for one night. Thinking about him right now only made her pussy wet.

Shelia

Shelia was a slim chick that wore her hair in long beautiful locks. She stood at 5'5 and weight 125 pounds. Her eyes were wide and her cheekbones sat high which made her look like an Egyptian woman. She had soft skin and did not have to wear a lot of make-up to make her look good. She had that beautiful natural look already. She always got compliments on how pretty she was. Shelia carried herself with dignity. She was a lovable person and her family and friends loved being around her. Shelia was a high-end real estate agent, so she was accustomed to the finer things in life, so when she met Marcus it was not like she wanted him for his money. She already had that (and he did too). It was like they say "love at first sight" and that is exactly how she felt when she first saw Marcus. She fell head over heels in love with him.

What shall I wear tonight? Shelia thought to herself as she took inventory of her expensive wardrobe in her large walk-in closet. She decided on a cute purple and white Dolce & Gabbana dress with white sandals. *I cannot forget my purple lace La Perla panties, just in case he wants to take my dress off of me,* she laughed to herself thinking about other naughty things that she would like for him to do to her. *Oh! This is going to be a good night. I have a date with a handsome man and we both have it going on. We would make a fabulous couple, but first I have to see if he really knows how to treat a woman, if he knows how to carry on a conversation and keep it interesting,* she thought. *He is going to love this dinner that I have prepared for him. It's my mother's best dish; she would always feed it to my father when she wanted something from him.* Shelia giggled a little and did a little spin in anticipation of her date.

Shelia went back to the kitchen to put the finishing touches on the meal. She pulled the last dish out of the oven, which was macaroni and cheese. She lit all the candles that she had placed throughout the living room. Then she dimmed the lights while the smooth voice of Luther Vandross flowed from her stereo. While walking back upstairs to her master bedroom she heard her cell phone ringing.

"Hello."

"Hey pretty lady, are you ready for me?"

Shelia was instantly turned on by the deep seductive sound of his voice. "Yes, I was headed up to my bedroom to put my clothes on."

"You don't need any clothes on, I'm your clothes."

"Like I told you early today, you are a mess!" The two of them started laughing and continued their conversation.

"Well, I'll see you in a few."

"Okay, see you when you get here." Shelia hung up the phone, turned on the shower, and poured the purple Love Spell nourishing bath and shower cream on her body. After showering, she emerged from the bathroom feeling refreshed. The shower had done her body well after the long day she'd had getting everything ready for this date. Shelia slathered the Love Spell lotion all over her body, before she slipped into her thong panties. After she dressed, she applied a little make-up—not much, and her lip-gloss. Shelia looked at herself in the mirror and was pleased with what she saw looking back at her.

I really look good tonight. This should definitely be a good date, she thought as she blew herself a kiss in the mirror and smiled. *I have not been on a date in a while now and I hope that I know how to keep a good conversation going myself. I might have lost my own touch after dealing with that fool Michael that I dated six months ago,* Shelia thought. *He really put a damper on me wanting to get into another relationship. Dealing with him was a trip.* Shelia shook her head to rid herself of that memory. Then she proceeded downstairs to make sure everything was to perfection. Right after Shelia set her best dishes out on the table, her doorbell rang.

Monica

"So how long do I have to be over there for this photo shoot?"

"You will be over there for two weeks." Monica was on the phone talking with her agent. She had to leave on Sunday to go to Paris to do a photo shoot. She wasn't happy about it. This was supposed to be her Sunday to spend with Sharon. They had planned to do church and afterwards have lunch at Carraba, but since Monica had to leave on such short notice, Sunday would have to be canceled for their girl's day out. Monica called Sharon to let her know that they would have to cancel their day.

"Hey, Shay, I was calling to let you know that I have to leave out of town on Sunday, so we will have to cancel our day."

"Girl, no! So where are you off to this time?" Sharon asked.

"To Paris."

"What? Get out of here! You have one of the best jobs ever. You get to travel everywhere, I'm so jealous!" Sharon gave a slight pout, but was still happy for her friend's success.

"Girl, please! You get to go out of town too Shay."

"Yeah, but not like you do."

"Yeah, but its spur-of-the-moment times like this when I don't like my job. It is okay when I know how my schedule is planned out six months ahead, but every so often my agent will throw in an unscheduled photo shoot. And of course, I have to go."

"Well, I know you're going to bring your bestest friend back a fabulous gift," Sharon teased.

"Now you know, every time I come back home you have something in one of my bags. You better enjoy the gifts that you'll be getting from me right now because after my niece or nephew gets here your gifts are over with." They both laughed. "So what did the doctor say? When is your due date?"

"Dec 31st."

"Wow" that's got to be hard for you, since your mom was born on that day."

"That's the same thing I said when he told me."

"Girl, I hope that while I'm gone you can get some rest. Don't worry about Darryl and his shit, you take care of you and the baby," Monica advised with concern.

"I know, and I will. I hate that we cannot do our Sunday date. I was really looking forward to it; we have some catching up to do. I was going to tell you everything that the doctor said," Sharon said, absently running her hand over the small bulge just beginning to show in her belly.

"Well, when I get back in town we will talk about everything. I know I'll be real busy while I'm away and I won't have a lot of time to just sit down and talk, but I will be calling and checking in on you."

"Have you spoken with your brother to let him know when you are leaving?"

"No, not yet, I was going to do that once I finished talking with you. Don't forget to come and check the house and mail for me."

I won't, you know I'm familiar with how everything goes when you are out of town or out of the country."

"Well, let me go so that I can call James and let him know where I will be, just in case he needs to get in touch with me."

"Okay girl, tell him I said hello. Be careful and know that I love you."

"I love you too, Shay," Monica said before disconnecting the call. Monica called her brother next to let him know that she had to go to Paris to do a photo shoot. Even though she was not there to help him with their mother and they were not close, she continued to send a check once a month to help her brother out with her expenses. She knew that it was wrong for her to let him take care of their mother all alone, but she just couldn't go back to Atlanta to live. And on top of that, she knew her mom probably wouldn't like her being at home with her.

"Harris and Johnson Law Firm, may I help you?"

"Yes, may I speak with James Harris?"

"May I ask who is calling?"

"This is his sister, Monica Harris."

"Just one moment please, let me get him."

"Hey sis, was going on?"

"Hey, I wanted to let you know that I have to leave for Paris on Sunday."

"When did this happen?"

"About an hour ago. It's one of those spur-of-the-moment things and I cannot get out of it."

"I understand, but you need to make it home 'cause your mom is not getting any better."

I know and I will. You know how mom and I can be when we get in the same room."

"Well it's time to put that behind and make it right 'cause you don't have a lot of time."

"James, not right now, I'm already upset because I have to leave like this, and to hear you with all of this isn't making it any better."

"I'm just sayin—"

"I know what you are saying," Monica said cutting him off. "I will call her once I get on the plane and check on her."

"Okay, you be careful and call me once you make it in."

"I will."

"Love you, sis."

"Love you too, bro. Oh! By the way, Shay told me to tell you hi."

"Tell her I said hello. How is she by the way?"

"About to become a mom."

"Oh shit! This has to be good, by whom?"

"I will fill you in on everything when I return, but I have to get going now."

"How long will you be in Paris?"

"Two weeks at the most."

"Okay, like I said, take care of yourself and I love you." They said their goodbyes and hung up.

Monica started packing her stuff in preparation for her trip. The following day she would have to go and get her hair fixed and her nails and toes done before her departure on Sunday. She wanted to talk with her mom, but not right now, she would really be depressed. Even though they did not see eye-to-eye she still felt bad for her mom. This cancer was really beating her and she did not know what to do. James was doing his best and it was not right for him to have to do everything and she not do anything. So she decided when she got back she would talk with her agent and reschedule her photo shoots so that she could visit and spend some time with her mom.

"Oh damn! I need to call and see if the vet can keep Diamond. Lord, I almost forgot about the dog. She really needs to go anyway because she is overdue for her wash and cut. Maybe I can ask my next door neighbor to keep her for me since he likes me and Diamond. I'll go and see if he can do me this favor," she mumbled under her breath. *Hope I don't have to give up any pussy for this,* Monica thought.

Monica left out of her house and walked next door to see if Max would keep Diamond for her while she was away for two weeks. Monica knocked on Max's door. She did not know how she would do this, but as she was getting ready to turn around and leave, Max opened up the door.

"Hey Max, were you busy?"

No, come on in. What's up with you?" Max asked as he stepped back and allowed her entry into his home.

"Well, I have a slight problem," Monica said following Max into his family room, taking a seat next to him on the sofa.

"Okay, go ahead. How can I help?"

"I have to leave town unexpectedly, my agent called me earlier today and I have to leave on Sunday to do a photo shoot in Paris. I need someone to take care of Diamond while I'm gone. I thought…"

Max held up his hands. "No need to say anything else. I'd love to keep Diamond for you. You know I'm crazy about that dog."

"You don't mind?" Monica asked relieved that her baby wouldn't have to be placed in a kennel.

"No, just tell me what I need to do."

"Thanks Max. I owe you big time."

" All I ask for is a date when you get back. Monica you know that I have always liked you, but you would never give me the time of day. I'm a pretty "cool" dude when you get to know me," he said smiling.

"You know what? It's a date. I would love to go out with you. I just have to go and see my mom first once I return because she isn't doing well. But after that, we will definitely have that date," Monica said smiling as a huge grin spread across Max's face.

"Okay, well just drop Diamond off tomorrow and I will take it from there."

"Thanks again Max, Oh! I will see if I can get her an appointment to see the vet while I'm gone. She needs a haircut and a bath."

"Cool."

Monica went back to her place to finish getting her things packed for Sunday. Then she called and made Diamond's appointment and hers to get her hair and nails done.

Sharon

As Sharon pulled into her driveway, she thought about days like this when she would come in and prepare dinner for her and Darryl. He really loved her cooking and he would always compliment her on how well she cooked. Tears formed in her eyes as she thought back on their recent situation. Sharon pulled herself together and emerged from the car. Once inside the house, she unpacked the grocery bags and sat down to rest for a while. She was tired from a long day. While Sharon was sitting on her lounge her telephone rang.

"Hello."

"Hey, baby girl."

"Hey, dad, how are you doing? I'm surprised to hear from you. I was going to call you once I got settled in."

"Oh, really?"

"Yeah, I have to talk with you about something."

"What is it baby girl?"

Sharon's voice began to tremble as she started telling her father that she was pregnant.

"Listen Sharon, I can hear it in your voice that you are afraid to tell me what is wrong, but I'm here to listen to you and not judge you. You are my baby girl and whatever it is, you can talk to me. I might not be your mother, but I'm your father and I love you."

"Dad, I love you too."

"So, what is it that has you so afraid to talk to me?"

"Dad, I'm pregnant."

"Okay, and you were afraid to tell me that I'm about to be a grandfather?"

That's because it's complicated."

"How complicated can it be?"

"Because my baby's father is "MARRIED."

"Oh baby girl, how did you let this happen?"

"I didn't know that he was married, I just found out myself the other day. Dad, it's a long story and I'm sorry for letting you down."

"You listen here just one minute. You have not let me down, it's just like you said it was complicated. I will not allow you to be hard on yourself. I'm here for you and this baby as long as I have breath in my body. Now what I want you to do is pull yourself together and not let this get you down. You are not the first for something like this to happen to and you won't be the last."

"Dad, you are the greatest. I've been so scared to come and tell you, but since Monica had to cancel our lunch date on Sunday I will come over after church and talk with you about everything."

"That will be fine. Baby girl, you keep your head up. You don't have anything to be ashamed of, whoever this man is that took part in this I want to meet him."

"Dad, I don't think that is going to happen because I told him I don't want to see him anymore."

"Sharon, I know that I cannot tell you how to live your life, but do not let this baby grow up not knowing who his/her father is."

"Dad, I'm just so angry at him right now that I don't want to see him. He could have told me that he was married."

Sharon never took Darryl to meet her father simply because she wanted to be engaged to Darryl when she did. Sharon was thirty-five years old and she was sick and tired of taking men to meet her father and yet never settle down. So whenever her dad asked if she was dating anyone she always said no.

"Well, I'll see you on Sunday and we can finish talking about all of this then."

"Okay, dad. See you Sunday. I love you."

"Love you too, baby girl."

Sharon hung up the phone and started to cry. She was so emotional from all of this that she could not pull herself together to get up and fix her taco salad. But she remembered that her doctor told her to make sure to take care of herself. *Let me get up and get something to eat so I can get a shower and a good night's rest,* Sharon thought to herself.

Once Sharon finished eating her taco salad she cleaned her kitchen and proceeded upstairs to her bedroom where she took a shower, turned on her TV, and watched the late nite show.

Tameka/Darryl

Once Tameka arrived home from Mom Essie's house she was worn out. She had heard everything that Mom Essie told her she needed to do, and the first thing she was going to do was pray to God to help her through this crisis. Yes, she wanted her marriage to work, but if her husband did not love her anymore there was nothing she could do about it. She could tell that Darryl had been by the house because some more of his clothes was missing from their closet.

I guess he has really made his choice about this whole situation, Sharon thought to herself. *What the hell is this?* There was a letter on the bed addressed to Tameka from Darryl. *I know good and damn well he did not have the nerve to leave me a letter instead of calling me to say what was on his mind. Darryl has really lost his damn mind, and I'm about to give him a piece of mine. This shit is about to go down. He will not continue to treat me like I'm some kind of stranger instead of his wife. I have loved this man too hard to allow him to mistreat me this way and think it is okay.* Tameka was livid.

Tameka picked up the phone and called Darryl's cell phone. She was about to give him a piece of her mind.

"Hello."

"Hey Darryl, I see that you left a letter here on the bed, what's this all about?"

"Did you not read it?"

"No, the hell I did not! Whatever you have to say to me you can voice it to me, not write me a damn letter like I'm some kind of stranger and not your wife. You know what Darryl, you are really acting like a "jackass" and I will not continue to take this kind of treatment from you. You are the one that went out and cheated on me, I can get your ass for adultery."

"I don't care if you do because you know it's some stuff that you have done to me that no one knows shit about, but I'm not going to go there. See, the letter that I left you was to tell you that I had been by to get some of my things and I was trying to see when was the next time you would be home so that we could sit down and talk. But since you want to act foolish and shit then bring it on."

"I see that you ran to your mom and told her everything."

Yes, that is *my* mom and not yours."

"Like I said, you are such a jackass. Look Darryl, I'll call you one day next week, but if I was you I would not just stop by here again because if you do, you might not be able to get in so the best thing for you to do is call before coming over."

"Try and change the locks, you bit—"

Before Darryl could finish his sentence Tameka hung up the phone in his face. *I cannot believe this man. He has really lost it!* "Lord, you are going to really have to help me through this, because if you don't, I just don't know what I might be capable of doing. I have given up too much for him to treat me this way. I put off my schooling so that he could get his business off the ground. I do know one thing, if it gets to the point of divorce he will not get this house and everything will be half—if not sixty-forty my way," Tameka spoke out loud.

Tameka looked at the wedding picture of her and Darryl that was on the countertop. She went over, grabbed it and threw it against the wall. The glass from the frame scattered all over the floor into pieces. She began to cry because that is what her life had just turned into—pieces. She fell to the floor and began to pray.

Heavenly Father, I come to you right now as humble as I can, asking that you guide and lead me in the right direction. I know that I have not been doing right by you, giving you the time that I should and reading your word, but right now my marriage is at odds and I need for you to help me. I don't know what to do and I'm seeking direction from you. You said 'look to the hills which cometh my help' and my help cometh from you lord. Lord, I'm your child and I need you right now, in your son Jesus name I pray, Amen.

I have faith that Jesus will be here to lead me in the right direction. I've got to get back in church starting Sunday, that is what I will be doing. It's time for a change and I'm about to make that change, Tameka thought with renewed faith and an uplifted heart.

Shelia/Marcus

"Well hello, pretty lady. You look beautiful."

"Thank you, and so do you. Come in and make yourself at home."

"Okay. What is that you have smelling so good?"

"You will see in a minute. Do you want something to drink?"

"Do you have Bud Light?"

"No, but I have wine, Budweiser, and Patrón."

"Hold up, I know a woman of your status does not take shots of Patrón?"

"Yes, I do, when me and my girls are hanging out at my house for our book club meetings."

"Oh, so you are in one of those book clubs too?"

"What do you mean by 'those book clubs'?"

"You know…" Marcus hesitated trying to find the right words.

"You know what, Marcus?" Shelia asked raising an eyebrow and folding her arms across her chest. "You may want to stop right there and let me know what you want to drink," she said with a laugh, rolling her eyes.

"Okay pretty lady, let me have Budweiser."

As Shelia was getting Marcus' drink she began putting their dinner out on the table. Shelia had prepared baked chicken, collard greens, macaroni and cheese, black-eyed peas, corn-bread, okra, a roast and peach pie for dessert. She placed everything on the table in her dining room. Marcus was amazed by her. She did not look like the type that could cook this type of food.

"What's wrong?"

"I'm just amazed at how you cooked all of this food," Marcus indicated waving his hand at the perfectly prepared food on the table.

"Who said that *I* cooked this?"

"Oh, I'm sorr—" Marcus stammered before Shelia cut him off.

"I was just kidding. Of course I cooked all of this, my mom made sure that I learned how to cook when I was little. I would get so upset with her because I wanted to be outside with the other kids playing, but she wasn't having it. I had to watch her three days out of the week on how to cook."

"This looks delicious," Marcus stated as he admired the feast on the table.

"Well, thank you! I might say myself that it is. Sit down so we can dig in." Shelia grabbed Marcus's hand and began to say the blessing. "Lord, we would like to thank you for this dinner and bless the hands that prepared it. Lord, we also want to thank you for being so good to us. These things we ask in your son Jesus name Amen."

"Amen," Marcus echoed giving Shelia's hand a slight squeeze.

During dinner Shelia and Marcus talked about everything from their childhood up to their lives to date.

Where they each went to college and the day-to-day challenges they had to overcome in order to make it.

"So Marcus why is it that a man of your stature doesn't have a woman?" Shelia asked taking a sip of her red wine.

"Who said I don't?"

Shelia looked shocked. She almost choked on her chicken.

"Gotch!" They both started laughing. "You know Shelia, I don't know. I was asking myself the same question earlier today. I think back on how my dad did my mom, and I can reflect from that. But some women out here are out for only one thing, and that is what they can get out of you. I try to be careful and I'm very particular about the kind of women that I deal with."

"So what kind do you deal with? The ghetto type or the sophisticated type?"

"Oh, so I see we are going to be on me all night. What about you? What type of man do you like?"

"I don't mind telling what kind of man I'm looking for, and yes, I'm looking because it gets lonely out here. I don't enjoy being alone all the time."

"You are right. Well, I'm looking for a woman with character. She has to know what she wants and strive to get it; not a begging woman. I don't mind helping my woman if she needs help, but I don't like a woman that begs just because she knows a brother has money. Then she has to have a sense of humor, not some stuck-up chick. She should also be smart, intelligent and a woman of God."

"A woman of God?" Shelia asked looking at him with a frown.

"Yes, she has to attend church. You need to have some word in your life so when things are not going right you know how to seek God first for your direction."

Shelia was impressed by this revelation. She was not expecting anything like this to come out of Marcus's mouth. She would have never thought that he would speak like this. She liked this man and was determined that she was going to keep him.

"So what about you, pretty lady, what do you look for? Thuggish type or the working man?"

"I want a man that does not look for a hand-out, someone that is hard-working and knows how to treat a woman. Of course he has to have a sense of humor, plus know how to cook, because I don't want to be the one doing the cooking *all* of the time. He should also be a God-fearing man."

"Okay, okay, I like that."

"I don't want someone who is out there trying to play games with me and every other woman out there. He needs to be honest, respectful and know what it takes to keep a good woman. I think that's why it's hard for me to have anyone because I require a lot. I don't mean to be that way, but sometimes you have to put a requirement on things."

Marcus was wondering if he would make it with Shelia because he knew he was a womanizer, but it was something that he was trying to stop. He wanted a relationship with someone, but it was hard for him to settle down with just one woman. He enjoyed going all of the time and most of the time they wanted to buy for him so he would never turn down the date. His mom always told him, "Son don't play with a woman's heart because one day it will catch up with you." He listened, but continued to be the "PLAYBOY" that he was.

"Hey, hey are you still with me? You looked like you were out of space," Shelia said, snapping Marcus out of his thoughts.

"Oh, I'm sorry. Did you have something on your mind that you wanted to say?"

"No, no I'm okay. Well, are you ready for the peach pie?"

"Girl, could I let this digest first?" Marcus stated patting his stomach. "If I get that pie right now I will fall asleep," he said with a smile.

"Well, what about another drink?"

"Patrón, that would be good."

Shelia cleared the dishes from the table and took everything back to the kitchen. She gave Marcus a shot of Patrón and went back to finish putting dinner away.

"So Shelia, I see that you like music too."

"Yeah, I do. If you want you can put in another CD," she called from the kitchen.

"I'm cool. You really have a nice home. How long have you lived here?"

I've been here for about five years now."

"Okay. So, you've been here by yourself all this time?"

"Yep. What about you, when will I be able to see your place?"

"The next time we have a date."

"Okay, I'm going to hold you to that."

As Shelia came back into the room with Marcus they continue their conversation drinking, laughing and enjoying each other's company. Marcus looked at Shelia and touched her face. A chill went through her body and she began to shiver from his touch.

"I'm sorry," he apologized.

"No, you're all right," Shelia sighed. She enjoyed the feel of his hands against her skin.

He began to touch her again, and this time he could not resist kissing her. They entangle into each other's arms kissing and touching. The next thing Shelia knew they were in her bedroom and she was coming out of those La Pearl panties that she had on.

Sharon

Sharon was watching TV when her phone rang. She looked at the caller ID, but the number came up WITHHELD. *I wonder who that could be?* she thought. *I hope Darryl's wife is not playing games calling me, but she did not have my home number when she called me the first time. It was on my cell phone so who the hell could this be?*

Sharon did not want to get any crazy ideals so she answered the phone and cursed whoever it was out before going back to watching TV. All she wanted was a relaxing night. After today she did not want anything getting her upset so she turned her ringer off so that she would not be disturbed. Sharon decided that she would talk with her baby. She wanted for this child to feel loved and she was going to make that happen no matter what.

"Hey little one, I know right now that things don't seem right but we are going to get through this. You did not ask to come here and this is not your fault, so what we are going to do is take care of each other," she continued as she rubbed her stomach. "You might not ever get to know your dad, but I'm going to be the best mother there is and you will also have the best grandfather there is. We will love you with everything that we have, and if your grandma was here, she would too. So while you are growing in me, we are going to grow together. I'm new at this so I need for you to be patient with me. I don't know what you are right now and I don't want to know until you get here, so for now, you are my 'little one' and I want you to know that I love you. So, you be strong in there and I'm going to be strong out here."

After Sharon finished talking with her baby she turned over to go to sleep, but before she could she remembered that she did not call Darryl. *I think I'll just wait until tomorrow. He's probably asleep right now.* She turned to say a pray before she fell off to sleep.

Our Father, my Heavenly Father, I come to you right now asking that you forgive me for my sins. I know what I have done is not right in your eyes, and that you are not pleased with it. But you said that you would cast our sins in the sea of forgiveness. Lord there's a baby involved now, and even though it came the wrong way I know that you don't make mistakes. I don't know what is suppose to come out of this, but I ask that you give me strength and that you guide me from this point on out. I need you right now Lord, show me the right way; how to live the rest of my life right. These things I ask in your son Jesus Name Amen.

Once Sharon finished praying she fell off to sleep.

Darryl

After Tameka hung up the phone in Darryl's face he went and took a shower. Darryl knew that Marcus would be hanging out late with this new chick so he decided to go into the den and watch TV. Darryl grabbed a beer out of the refrigerator, made a sandwich and began watching TV.

"Damn! That Tameka knows she can get on my last nerves talking about changing the locks and shit. I can see how this is going to turn out with her. This is the kind of mess I did not have to put up with, with Sharon. She was not a control freak like that wife of mine, but I will not have to put up with this after the divorce," Darryl said to himself.

Darryl started thinking about Sharon and wondered what she was doing. He really did miss her, but he had already made up in his mind that he was not going to let her get away from him. *I really do love that girl. She could really make me laugh. I bet right now she is either reading a book, or looking at television. I'm a fool for hurting such a good person like her, she really deserves the best,* he thought to himself.

I wonder if she's still up? If I call her I can block the number so that she will not be able to call me back. I just want to hear her voice to see if she sounds okay. This situation has to get better, it cannot go on like this, plus mom wants to meet her. I got to get her to talk with me some kind of way, he thought.

Darryl picked up the phone to dial Sharon number *67223-7506. He blocked the number out so that if she tried to call back she could not.

"Hello. Hello. Stupid ass don't call here anymore."

Darryl started smiling when he heard her voice. He really did miss this girl. "Yep, she is okay. That's Sharon, the only time you could get her to cuss you out was to do some shit that she doesn't like," he spoke out loud. Darryl hung up the phone and continued to watch the TV until the TV started watching him.

Monica

This has been one of the worst days of my life, things are not going right. First, it starts to rain and I need to get out of here to get going, my plane leaves at 5 o'clock. Max came and got Diamond and took her to get herself together. When they returned, Diamond looked like they tried to take every piece of her hair off of her body. On top of everything else, my brother called talking about coming to see mom because she is not doing well at all.

I hope that I have everything because if not, I will just have to get what I need when I get there. I hate when this kind of shit happens, having to leave on such short notice, but this is something that I chose to do with my life so I have to deal with it. Maybe one day while traveling all around I might just run into the right man, settle down and get married. That would be the day I would love to see, and I think everyone else would too. Let me call GI-GI and see have they left yet to come and get me.

"Hey GI-GI, are you on your way? So I will know to have my stuff at the door for the chauffeur."

"Yeah, we are right down the street," GI-GI replied.

"Okay, see you in a few."

"Do you have everything taken care of while you're gone?"

"Yeah, Diamond is next door and Sharon will be checking on everything else for me."

"Good. Well we're pulling up so open the door."

"Okay."

Once GI-GI pulled up in the limo the chauffeur got out and proceeded to Monica's house to get her bags. He then took them to the limo as Monica locked her door and followed behind him. She knew that this would be a long ride to the airport. GI-GI could really talk, and sometimes she just didn't know when to shut up. Monica loved GI-GI a lot, they have been through some stuff together and GI-GI always looked out for her when it came to a photo shoot. But Monica just didn't like it when she discussed other model's business. So Monica put on her fake smile and pretended like she was interested in what GI-GI was talking about.

Shelia/Marcus

Shelia was on her back with her legs wrapped around Marcus's back. She had an arch in her back and she felt like she was getting a cramp, but at that moment she did not care. She was feeling so good from Marcus's touch that the only thing she could do was scream out loud.

Marcus had kissed Shelia from her head down to her toes. He had touched every inch of her body with his tongue. Her pussy was so wet she was about to cum. He licked her pussy until her nails dug inside of his skin. He was loving every bit of it because he knew once he stuck his dick inside of her she was going to be cumming all over.

"Marcus you feel soooo good," Shelia moaned.

"So do you, Shelia."

"Put your dick inside of me before I cum, I need you inside me."

"You want me inside that pussy?" Marcus teased while rubbing the head of his dick against her clit.

Sharon was moaning in pleasure anticipating what was coming. "Oh yes I want you, I want you bad. I need to feel you and you need to feel me." Marcus spread

Shelia's legs wide open and put his nine inch dick inside of her. Before he knew it, Shelia was screaming his name.

"I didn't know your pussy was going to feel this good, Shelia. I don't want to cum yet. Girl, you are working that pussy."

"I don't want to cum either, just don't stop. You are sooooo good."

"Turn over, I want you every way I can have you." Shelia turned over and Marcus began to fuck her from the back, and she was loving every bit of it. He grabbed her breast and kissed her all over her back. When Marcus started kissing her back Shelia could not hold it any longer, she came over and over. Once Marcus felt her cum he began to cum. They were both so tired from the lovemaking that within minutes they were asleep, with Shelia in his arms.

Marcus woke up around three in the morning but he was not about to drive all the way back to the other side of town. He looked over at Shelia and saw how beautiful she looked. He wondered if she looked this beautiful every night while she slept. He had to use the bathroom so he got up to go.

Shelia felt him moving and woke up. "Are you okay?" she said yawning.

"Yeah baby, I'm fine, just going to the bathroom. Lay back down, I can find it." When Marcus returned Shelia was laying there with this look on her face that was saying 'I'm ready to go again'.

"Would it be okay if I stay over? I don't feel like taking that ride all the way back to the other side of town," Marcus asked.

"Sure. Can I get you anything? There are towels in the bathroom, if you need it."

"No, the only thing you can get for me right now is some more of that good pussy," Marcus said with a grin.

"That's not a problem."

Shelia pushed Marcus down. "I hope you are prepared for what I'm about to do to you because you are going to be begging me to stop."

"Baby, you do whatever you have do because I'm going to enjoy it all." Shelia went down on Marcus and sucked him until her jaws were so tight they went numb. She couldn't feel them.

"Oh baby, please stop! Please stop!"

"Oh, so you want me to stop?" Shelia laughed.

"Yes, I want to taste you all over again."

"Well, come and get it then."

Marcus put Shelia on her back, spread her legs, and licked her until she came. He licked all of her juices and once he finished, he put that nine inch dick back inside her. They made love all night long until they were so exhausted they couldn't go any longer. They both fell asleep in each other's arms, by then the sun was coming up.

Tameka

As the sun was coming through the window, Tameka rolled over to see what time it was. She had already planned on going to church today so she had a couple of hours left before she would get up. Last night was a crazy night and she was not going to let Darryl get to her today. She had already prayed about this situation with him and today was going to be a new beginning for her. Tameka turned the radio on next to her bed and set the dial to Hallelujah FM. She listened to the song "Stand" and the words hit her right on the spot. She pulled herself together and got out of bed. That song put some energy in her just that fast. She started singing the lyrics along with Donnie McClurkin.

I have always liked his music, his voice is so unique. He tells his story in a book about his life and the things that happened to him and look at how he turned out, so it shouldn't be hard for me to get myself together, she thought. Tameka began to pray while she entered into the bathroom. Lord, *help me to be strong to endure what is going on in my life right now. I know that I have not served you the way I should have, but Lord I need your strength to help me. I do know this, I will look to the hills which cometh my help and my help comes from you, so Lord, I'm going to wait on you and look for direction from you, Amen.*

Let me get in this shower so I can get ready for church. I don't know what to wear, some churches don't like for you to come as you are. They want to continue the tradition like when I was growing up. One thing my mom always said, 'If you train a child when they strayed away they will come back,' and she was right about that. I might just go over to her church, Faith and Hope Deliverance Baptist Church. Yes, I think that I will pay Pastor Ronald Hall a visit today, Tameka thought with a smile, happy about her decision to visit her mother's church.

After Tameka got out of the shower she went into her closet and pulled out her beige Gucci pant suit along with her Gucci shoes and handbag, she applied some Mary Kay makeup—not too much, just a little to give her a little enhancement. Then she brushed her hair, and looked at herself in the mirror. "Yes! I look marvelous," she said as she gave her reflection a wink. She grabbed her Gucci shades and walked out of the house. "This is the day that the Lord has made and I will rejoice in it." She got into her car and headed to Faith and Hope Deliverance Baptist Church.

Marcus

As Marcus rolled over he knew that he was not in his own bed because of the way the sun was hitting his eyes. Marcus opened one eye and looked over at Shelia. Just like last night she was beautiful even when she slept. He was really feeling Shelia, but was trying to convince himself that it would not work; that he could not wake up with the same woman on the side of him *every* morning.

"Hey pretty lady, wake up."

"Something wrong? Do you need me to get you anything?"

"Yeah, can I get a washcloth and towel? Or you can just point me in the right direction and I'll get it myself."

"No, I can get it for you."

"Thanks! Look, pretty lady, once I finish taking a shower I'm going to head home, but I want you to know that I had a great time with you last night and I hope that we can see each other again. Maybe this time I can cook for you, but I have to warn you, my cooking is nothing like yours."

"That's okay, as long as I get another date we will worry about the cooking later."

"Cool."

Marcus went into the bathroom to take a shower. He was really feeling Shelia. He knew this because he had already given her a pet name. She was just his type. It had been a while since he had found a woman of her character. He had to tell Darryl about this woman and he knew that his friend was going to be hard on him because he never bragged about a woman from the first date. Marcus emerged from the bathroom with the towel wrapped around him. His body looked so good that Shelia wanted to start all over again with him, but she did not want to overdo it. Marcus put on his cloths and headed to the door.

"Hey pretty lady, want to walk me out? I will not feel right leaving here without seeing your pretty face at the door and getting a kiss from you."

"Sure, let me get my robe and I will be right with you."

When Shelia reached the door Marcus lifted her chin to look into her eyes. "Hey, don't look like that. We will see each other again. I need to get home and check on some things, but I will give you a call today."

"I understand, I need to catch up on some work today too, plus I need some more rest. You wore me out last night and this morning."

"I wore *you* out? Shit, you got me tired as hell. I'm going to have to get some rest, but I know my boy is not going to let me rest. He is going to talk about me like a dog, and it's all your fault."

"How? What did I do? Not a thing."

"You put that good pussy on me, but I'm not complaining. I loved every bit of it."

"I bet you did, and trust me, I loved every bit of you," Shelia replied reaching up to give him another kiss.

"I'll call you later."

"Okay."

Marcus hadn't had a night like this one in a while and he really did enjoy it. Marcus started his truck, put in his Marvin Gaye CD and pulled out of Shelia's driveway. On his way home he was consumed with thoughts of her. *Now that was a night. I really did enjoy Shelia from the conversation to the lovemaking; she really has it going on. She's a smart woman, can cook, and can definitely make love. I got to stop letting that shit that my father did to my mom interfere with my relationships with women and how I treat them. Right now, Shelia does not know it but I am Philogyny, and I don't want to hurt her. I may just have to do what my mom told me a long time ago and that is to talk with someone about this, because I'm not about to mess this up with this woman. There's just something about her, she's just different from all the rest,* Marcus thought.

Man, Darryl is really going to dog me out when I get in the house. I told him that I would not be staying out all night, that this one was just like the rest of the dates that I've had, but it turns out that I was wrong as hell. This one was nothing like the rest of them. Well, he really can't say too much, I'll just get back on his ass with Sharon and Tameka and that will shut him up. I hate it for my boy, he is a good guy, he just got into a bad situations. I just hope that Tameka doesn't do anything stupid like try and kill my boy when she finds out that Sharon is having his baby.

By the time Marcus was pulling up in his driveway his cell phone rang.

"Hello."

"Hey Marcus, just wanted to make sure that you made it home."

"Girl, you know you just wanted to hear my voice, you miss me already? I'm not going anywhere."

"Don't flatter yourself. I was just making sure you made it in alright. I know that you were a little weak when you left here."

"Okay, okay so we got jokes now." They both laughed.

"No, I do not have jokes. I just wanted to tell you that I really did enjoy last night. I have not had a night like that in a long time and I hope to see you again soon."

"You will definitely see me again. I had a great time myself last night. I was thinking about it while driving home, you really know how to entertain your company."

"It depends on who the *company* is, but I just wanted to let you know how I felt. I will let you get yourself settled and I will give you a call later on today."

"Okay, pretty lady. Talk to you later."

Darryl

The ringing of the phone woke Darryl up out of his sleep, he had fallen asleep watching TV. It was around one o'clock when he looked at his watch to see what time it was, and who could be calling him this time of the morning.

"Hello," he answered sleepily.

"Hi Darryl."

"Sharon?"

"Yes, it's me. I need to talk with you about something."

"Okay, go ahead."

"I need to know why. Why did you lie to me and why did you cheat on your wife?"

"Sharon let me explain something to you. It was never my intention to cheat on my wife."

"Say what?"

"Hold up, let me say what you need to hear. When we first met in the mall that day, Tameka and I had just had a fight. We had been going at it for months now and I just needed to get out of the house. I came to the mall to clear my head, not to run into you. But once we exchanged numbers and started talking I could not find myself telling you that I was married, because by that time I had fallen in love with you and did not want to stop seeing you. I was enjoying every minute that I spent with you, because what you were giving me I was not getting at home. And I'm not talking about the lovemaking. I'm talking about all of it.

"I was not happy at home and I was planning on leaving before you came into the picture, it just made it so much easier when we got together. You made me laugh, and you listened to me when you didn't have to. All I got from home was complaining. It was always something. Somewhere over the years we had lost the connection that we had, and I know she wasn't happy either. I know that this does not make up for the hurt that I caused you, but I want you to know that I LOVE YOU, and that will never change. I also want you to know that I want to be a part of my child's life. It would kill me if I could not be. Sharon, you are a great woman and any man is *lucky* to have you. I just hope that one day you can forgive me and that we can be friends."

"Darryl, this is a hard pill to swallow and it's going to take some time for me to get over this. This is not like you took my car without my permission and wrecked it; you have taken a year of my life and wrecked *it*. Now I'm having your baby, and you are still married. This is just too much."

"I know, I know. I don't know how things are going to work out but I do know that I'm not giving up on you. I have spoken with my mom about this."

"What? I know you got to be out of your mind."

"No, my mom is cool. She did tell me that I was wrong because of how I lead you on, and for going outside of my marriage. She respects the decisions that I make and that she will always be there for me. She told me that my father would be very upset with me right now because they did not raise me this way. It was never my intention to cause you any hurt. It was foolish of me, and all I can say is that I'm sorry. My mom wants to meet you. I know that you will not agree to it, but I did tell her that whenever I spoke with you I would let you know. I told her we were not speaking at the moment, and she said she doesn't blame you for that, but she does want to know the woman who is carrying her grandchild."

Sharon started laughing because her father had said the same thing about Darryl; that he wants to meet the man who has his daughter pregnant.

"What is so funny? I'm not joking about this."

"No, I'm laughing because when I told my dad what happened he said the same thing. That he wants to meet you. I told him that I was so mad at you right now that I didn't want to see or hear from you. He does not want his grandchild gowning up not knowing who his/her father is."

"You got to be joking."

"No, I'm not."

"Well, you let him know that when you are ready to forgive me and we can become friends out of all of this, I will be ready to meet him."

"Darryl, I just don't know right now. I cannot just forget that this has happened. I have to have some time. I cannot promise you anything at this moment."

"I understand what you are saying and I can respect your feelings on this. I will not cause you any problems, but you can always call me if you need me. Right now I'm staying with Marcus so if you cannot reach me on my cell you know where I am. I'm really sorry for all of this, you deserve so much better."

"I'm sorry too. Good night, Darryl."

"Good night, Sharon. Take care and just don't forget to call me if you need me."

As Darryl hung up the phone he got up to get a glass of water. He was glad that he had spoken with Sharon and was hoping that she would soon forgive him and they could become one. That's when he noticed that Marcus was not at home and it was two in the morning. He started laughing to himself. *I knew he had the hots for this one, trying to make like he is Mr. Hardcore knowing all the while he was feeling this one,* Darryl thought. But Darryl could not get Sharon's voice out of his head. He was missing her every minute and all he wanted to do was hold her and rub on her stomach. *I got to get this shit right, if not, I'm going to be lost without her. At least I know right now that she is okay.* With that, Darryl lay back down and went to sleep with a smile on his face thinking about the woman that he loves carrying his baby.

Sharon

Sharon felt a little better now that she had spoken with Darryl. She needed to hear what he had to say when she asked the question. She still loved him and most of all, she wanted to be in his arms right now, but she knew that was not going to happen under the circumstances. This was not supposed to be happening to her, not like this, this is not how she planned on becoming a mother.

I really do miss him. I just don't know if I could ever trust Darryl again, not after the way he played me. Darryl should have manned-up and told me the truth, but instead, he continued to lie every day that we were together. I should have seen some kind of sign, but I was so blinded by "love" that I could not see anything. I want him to be a part of this child's life. I don't want my baby not knowing who helped give him life then hate me for not letting Darryl be a part of his or her life. It's just going to take some time. I don't know what the hell is going on between him and that wife of his, but if he stays with her I do know one thing, my child will not be going to their house and be mistreated by that crazy woman. She's already called me and there's no telling what she might do to my child, so I'm going to do what I know is best and make sure that if he stays with her, my child will not go there. I did enjoy talking with him tonight and I pray that everything turns out for the best. Darryl is a good man, he just made a terrible mistake by committing adultery. We've all sinned and fallen short of the glory of God. He needs to ask God to forgive him and then do what is best for him and go on with his life. Sharon's mind was consumed with thoughts about her situation with Darryl and the baby. Then she decided to pray.

Lord, help Darryl to correct the mistakes that he has made. Forgive him for the sin that he has committed and also, forgive me for being a part of that sin. I know that we all do things that are not pleasing to you, so help us Lord to learn to do things that are good and not bad. I know that we cannot change overnight but as we continue to go to church, seek you, pray, and ask for guidance then we will know how to live the life that you want us to. Lord, I know that a child has been conceived out of this mess, no, I'm not going to call it a mess but this situation. I pray that you still protect my child and let my child know that he or she is not a mistake, but a blessing. Even thought it was wrong for the way it happened. I pray in your son Jesus name Amen. After Sharon finished praying she smiled, rubbed her stomach, and fell asleep.

Monica

"Girl, that was some kind of flight. I'm glad that we are off that plane because I was getting afraid, looks like we kept having some kind of problems. All I want to do now is get to our hotel, take a shower, and lay down. I need to rest my head."

"You got to be kidding me, we are in Paris and you want to take a shower and lay down? I think not, we are going to take a shower and go have some drinks before we start to work. After today we have a lot of work to do and not a lot of time to play. So it's going down tonight!" GI-GI exclaimed excitedly.

"GI-GI, I hate it when I have to do these last minute shoots, it just messes up everything for me. I have to rearrange my whole life. From now on could you at least ask me before you go making any deals?"

"Monica! What is up with you? You have had this bad taste of attitude all day. I'm looking out for you. All I try to do is get you the best that I can and you give me attitude."

"I'm sorry, but I have a lot on my mind. I can't help but think about my mom. She's really sick and I'm here when I should be there with her."

"I thought you and your mom didn't get along?"

"We don't, but she is still my mother. Am I not supposed to give a shit about her because we don't get along? In case you forgot my mom has cancer!" Monica spat while rolling her eyes at GI-GI's lack of empathy.

"Look, I'm sorry, you know that I didn't mean it that way. I know you still love your mom regardless of the relationship that you all have. I just want you to relax and pull yourself together. We are going to go out, get something to eat and drink, and get the rest of these two weeks over with so we can get you back home to be with your mom."

"Don't forget the shopping."

"Oh shit, that's right. We cannot forget to bag up before we leave, but I promise you from now on I will see how everything is going with you before I make anymore off-the-schedule shoots," GI-GI promised.

"Thanks GI-GI."

"You're my girl, I can't afford to lose you so I'm going to see that you are taken care of and keep you happy so that you can stay with our company."

"Girl, I'm not going anywhere."

"Well, let's get out of here and go have some fun."

As the girls proceeded to head out of their hotel room walking side-by-side talking and laughing, they ran into the most gorgeous man.

Tameka

When Tameka walked up to the church her heart started beating fast. She hadn't been here in two years and she felt ashamed at this moment. She did not tell her mom that she was coming because she wanted to surprise her. When she walked inside the church she was greeted by the greeters that stood at the entrance of the church. They were all wearing black and red with smiles on their faces. After passing the greeters, she walked inside of the sanctuary and looked around for her mom. Tameka did not see her, so she walked down the aisle and sat in the middle pew. While sitting there and waiting for the service to begin someone came up behind her and tapped her on her shoulder.

"Hey Mom, you scared me there for a minute," she smiled giving her mom a hug.

"Sorry baby, I'm so glad to see you here. I didn't know that you would be here today."

"I didn't either, but I'm here now."

"Mrs. Green told me she saw you come in and she came and got me from the fellowship hall."

"Okay, I see some people here still know me," Tameka whispered.

"Yes, they do, baby."

"So when did you get back home? You didn't call and say you were back or anything."

"It was late when I got in, all I did was take a bath and get in the bed because I knew that I had to be here today to usher. Look, I got to go back to get ready before we start, but let's do lunch after church so we can talk."

"That would be great. I will meet you at your house afterwards."

"Okay, love you baby."

"Love you too, mom."

Once Pastor Hall walked out from the side door on to the pulpit he greeted the congregation, everyone stood and started to clap. This was their way of greeting their pastor on Sunday mornings. Tameka felt out of place because she really didn't know what to do, but she just followed along with everyone else. Once everyone sat down the choir begin to sing "I Will Sing Hallelujah." They sounded like angels singing; people were shouting and falling out. The choir was so anointed that chills begin to come over Tameka's body and she began to shake in her seat. Once everybody calmed down, the Pastor stood up and asked if they could take out their Bibles and turn to Luke Chapter 17, Verse 32. The message was "Remember Lot's Wife." All Tameka could think was, *Oh my God, could he be talking to me today? If so, I came to the right church today,* she thought. Tameka listened as Pastor Hall spoke on how we cannot let go of the past and that is what keeping us from moving forward and getting the blessing that God has for us. Pastor Hall spoke on how we like to be slaves to our memories and that we just cannot forget, "Whatever mistakes that you have made, let it go, you cannot not fix it, and whomever that person is that hurt you—let it go." He told them that Lot's wife turned into a "pillar of salt" because she could not let the past go, she looked back because she wanted to see what was going on, she just had to take one last look. That's what happens to us, we are so hooked on the past that we cannot see our future and what God has for us. As long as we look back we are walking into all kinds of trees and walls, not knowing that "The Best Is Yet To Come."

"Oh my God, this Pastor has really preached the word today," Tameka spoke silently. *This is what I needed because I thought that my life was over just because of what happened between Darryl and me. If this is what he wants then he can have it because, "The Best Is Yet To Come For Me." I will not dwell on the past anymore, and I will not treat him badly because I refuse to miss the blessing that God has for me. The things that are not good for us we try to hold on to, not knowing that we should just let it be, but what I have received today from Pastor Hall is confirmation that I will be back again. Let me go and speak to him, I know that he might not remember me, but I just want him to know that he has really blessed me today with this sermon,* Tameka thought as she made her way through the crowded sanctuary to the front of the pulpit.

"Hello, Pastor Hall."

"Tameka, is that you? You are really looking like your mother now," he said as he gave Tameka a warm hug.

"Thank you Pastor, I just wanted to come and speak with you to let you know how you really blessed my soul today."

"Well, you know me, I'm old but I still know how to touch the souls of the people. It really makes me feel good when I know that I have blessed someone with the Lord's Word. It brings me great joy to know that I have saved another soul. I love what I do because a lot of people are out there hurting and when a person walks in those doors on Sunday morning, I want to be the one that has given them some hope on what is going on in their lives."

"Well, you really help me today."

"I'm glad that I did. If you want I can pray for you."

"That would be great. So when do you want me to come back by?"

"Baby I'm talking about right now. When God tells me to do something, I move then."

"Okay, I'm ready," Tameka said, taking a deep breath.

"Let's bow our heads and compose our hearts. *Father God, we come to you right now asking you to forgive us for our sins, we ask that you let any anger or hate that we have in our hearts be removed. We know that you are a God of all things and that you can do the impossible, so we ask that you move anything that is not of you from around us. We have been hurt by loved ones and we want to be able to forgive them, but in order to do that we've got to let go of the past that we are holding on to. Father, we love you, and we want to start right now this day of the hour to give you the glory and honor and start walking in your will and not ours. These and other things we ask in your precious son Jesus Name Amen."*

"Amen."

"Thank you Pastor, I will see you on next Sunday."

"I'll be looking for you. Tell your mother I said hi, and I'm sorry that I didn't get a chance to speak with her today like I normally do, but let her know that it was for a good reason," the Pastor said with a smile.

"I sure will." As Tameka began to walk out of the church her spirits felt so much better. She knew then that she had been sent there today by God to receive the word that was delivered on today. Once she got into her car her cell phone was ringing. She answered it feeling alive and renewed.

"Hello."

"Hey baby, I thought that you would be here when I got home so we can have lunch?"

"I'm on my way. I spoke with Pastor after church, that's why I'm running late. Oh...he told me to tell you he missed talking with you today, but it was for a good reason."

"Well, if he was talking with my daughter then it was for a good reason."

"Well, I'll be there shortly. I'll see you when I get there."

"Okay, baby."

Marcus/Darryl

It was morning when Marcus walked into his house. He knew once his boy saw him it was going to be on. He found Darryl asleep on the couch with a smile across his face.

"Darryl! Wake up, man. Hey man, wake up!"

Darryl turned over and saw Marcus standing over him. "Hey man what's up?"

"You. Why are you in the den sleeping? You must have had company last night?"

"Nope, is it morning already?"

"Yes!"

"So I thought you weren't staying out all night? Remember what you told me, 'you know how I do it'," he stated mocking his friend. "She must have done you good," Darryl said, laughing at his friend.

"Hey man, don't start with that. You know me, I'm the man," Marcus said brushing off his collar and tilting his head to the side.

"Well, you were not the man last night."

"Look, girl got it going on. You know, I'm really feeling her. There's something unique about her. I have not though about a woman on my drive home since college."

"Yeah, I remember Linda. Man, you were crazy about that girl. She really did you bad. You know, when you are a freshman in college dating a senior, you think you got it going on, but all the while your ass is being played," Darryl said.

"Yeah, she played my ass good, but that's okay 'cause look at a brother now—a sexy, top-notch dentist, and ladies man with a pocket full of money," Marcus replied flexing.

"Whatever happened to her? Didn't she marry that football player that whipped your ass that Friday night? I'll never forget that night."

"Me either, man. I was so embarrassed that Monday morning in Chemistry class that I left and went back to our dorm. She married old dude but he ended up leaving her ass with four kids and shit. The last time I saw her she was looking bad. They said that she got on drugs after he left her and their kids went to her mom, but her mom ended up dying so I guess she got herself back on track after that. She could've had me, but nooooo...she wanted to be a player."

"Okay, tell me about last night, that's what I want to hear."

"It was good. She made a mean dinner, and we had good conversation and stuff. I really thought it was going to be like; 'OK tell me all about you, and how much money you make,' you know, the kind I usually end up with—clothes so damn tight and shit trying to make their breast look bigger and all that kind of stuff. But this woman was just like I said, she is unique. It doesn't take a lot to make her look good, and she has such good character and I like her spirit."

"Sooo, what you are telling me is that you are going to give this chic a chance, not some six month relationship?" Darryl asked raising an eyebrow.

"That's exactly what I'm saying."

"Then in that case, I'm proud of you and happy for you. I know how you get when you get close to a woman, so you are either going to seek help or let that shit go about your dad."

"I've made up my mind that I'm going to see someone about my problem."

"Why don't you go see Sharon, that *is* her line of work, you know?"

"Hell nah, she will think that I'm trying to get up in your business, and with me being your best friend she would never go for that."

"Look, set up an appointment. All Sharon knows is your first name and if she tells you that she cannot see you then try someone else."

"I'll think about it."

"So, did you hit that ass?"

"I don't kiss and tell I cannot believe you asked me that shit."

"I'm your boy, you know how we do it."

"I know. That's why for right now I'm keeping my shit to myself so I won't mess things up, but I will tell you this, she is sexy as hell naked," Marcus said with a smile, rubbing his chin. Both men started laughing. They talked for about two hours before Marcus told Darryl that he was going to lie down for a while. "But before I go, what went on with you last night?"

"Man, I had it out with Tameka's crazy ass, and Sharon ended up calling me. We talked for a good while, and her dad wants to meet me. We both laughed about that because I told her my mom wants the same thing."

"So you two are getting along good so far?"

"I wouldn't say that. I still have to give her some more time because she is still pretty upset with me. Marcus, man, I really fucked up with this one. I love this woman and I want to be with her. I need to make this right. I just need time to sort things out. I don't want to rush her, but I also don't want to lose her. Tameka is a closed chapter for me. You all just don't know what I've had to deal with over the last couple of years. It has not only been me stepping outside of our marriage, but Tameka has too."

"You are shitting me?"

"No, I'm not. There's a lot that I have not told you or my mom because I wanted to keep this private and not bring shame to her. But the way she is carrying on about what I've done, you would have thought she has been an angel all this time. This is going to be a tough divorce."

"What if she does not want one?"

"I'm still filing for one anyway."

"Well, like I've said before, I got your back. So are you in for the day?"

"No, I'm about to go and visit with mom."

"Cool, I'll see you later." With that Marcus went up to his room to take a nap. He really did want to call Shelia. He was missing her already, but he didn't want to appear soft, so he decided to call her once he woke up from his nap.

Sharon

When Sharon woke up she felt pretty good. She got out of bed, went into her bathroom to wash her face and brush her teeth before going downstairs to make herself something to eat. She was going to see her dad today. She thought about her lunch date that she was supposed to be having with her best friend Monica. She wondered what she was doing right now since she had not spoken with her. *Oh! I almost forgot! I need to go and check her mail today after I leave dad's house. She never did tell me who was keeping Diamond this time. I wonder if she took her to the vet? I'm going to send her a text and find out where Diamond is staying,* she thought. Sharon grabbed her Blackberry phone and sent Monica a text to find out about her dog.

Monica sent Sharon a reply text letting her know that Max was keeping Diamond until she returned from her trip. *Well, that's one thing I don't have to worry about,* Sharon thought. Sharon went into her kitchen and prepared herself some breakfast so that she could take her vitamins. She wanted to do just what her doctor had told her so that everything would be okay with the baby. Once Sharon finished with breakfast she went to take a shower. While taking a shower she noticed how her stomach was beginning to grow. Tears welled up in her eyes because this was not how things were suppose to go. She was supposed to have her husband with her as they watched her stomach grow together. They were supposed to be painting the baby's room and picking out clothes together, not one parent married and the other by herself. Sharon began to get dressed. She put on a pink Dereon sundress with her white Dereon sandals. She accessorized it with the shades and purse. She looked at herself in the mirror and couldn't help but think, *Damn, how could I have been so foolish? This is the worst thing that has ever happened to me. My baby is not a mistake, I will never think that, but I should have been more aware of the things that were going on in this relationship with Darryl. He would sometime stay overnight once or twice, I guess that's why I didn't think anything was strange. And he would take me to the house where he and Marcus stayed, but now I see that was his cover up. I could kill him for this. There is not a chance in hell that I would allow him into my life again. Marcus was with this shit all along. He knew that Darryl was married and never said a word. I guess both of them play the same game, the only thing is that Marcus is not married. Just wait till I see him, I'm going to give him a piece of my mind too. That red bastard! I could kill his ass too,* Sharon thought with a frown.

Sharon proceeded to walk out of her house to her car. She was headed to her dad's for the day. She wanted to spend as much time with him as possible considering how her mother died. While driving to her dad's she thought back on the day that her mother passed away.

It was a murky day and the wind was blowing very heavy. Sharon and her mom were very close, they would talk about everything, and they spent a lot of time together when she was growing up. Her mother was so proud of her because she was the daughter that did not give her parents any trouble. Whatever they told her she could or could not do, she would obey. She thought back to the day when she graduated from high school, how her mother beamed with so much pride. She made sure that all of her family members were there to witness this day, she gave her the biggest party there was. But when she thought about the day that her mother died, tears came to her eyes. Sharon was at work when she got the phone call from her dad telling her to come to the hospital. Her mom had a heart attack. Sharon ran out of the office and headed to the hospital. Once she got there she asked the receptionist at the desk about her mother. She told Sharon where to go. When she saw her dad sitting in the waiting room with his head hanging down she ran to him, hugging him as tightly as she could. She asked her dad what had happened and he explained everything to her. They both waited for the doctor to come out and let them know what the results were. They looked up and saw the doctor walking towards them. They both stood up and waited to see what he had to say, but they were not expecting the news that he gave them. Sharon's mom had died while on the operating table. Sharon fell into her father's arm crying. Her dad was trying to keep his composure, but it was too hard for him to do. His wife for over thirty-eight years was gone out of his life, leaving him and their daughter.

Sharon brought herself back to reality when she heard a car horn blowing. She had just run a red light almost causing an accident. She was so nervous that she pulled over on the side of the road to get herself together. "Lord, what was I thinking? I almost killed myself, my baby, and someone else," she spoke out loud. "All of this is just too much to handle. How am I going to do this without my mom? Let me get to my dad's house before I end up doing something else stupid. I've got to stay in control for me and my baby. This is going to be a long nine months, but I'm going to make it. I do know one thing, if it's a girl her middle name will be after my mom."

After Sharon pulled herself together she started her car and headed towards her dad's house. She drove for about another fifteen minutes before she pulled up in his driveway.

Monica/GI-GI

"Girl, this is the best wine I've had in a while, what is it called again?" Monica asked fingering the beautiful bottle.

"La boutelle de vin. Let me order us another bottle to go with our dinner."

The ladies had gone to Galvin Bistrot de Luxe on Baker Street to have dinner. Both ladies ordered the grilled sirloin steak with beamaise sauce.

"Everything is soooo...good."

"Yes, it is, but you better watch yourself with that wine. It will sneak up on you."

"That's what I need, for something to sneak up on me, and I need it to be a man." Both ladies started laughing at the statement that Monica had just made.

"By the way GI-GI, who is the designer that I will be advertising their cloths for?" Monica asked taking another sip of her wine.

"He is someone new and he lives here. That is one reason why we are in Paris. His name is Desire' Laird."

"Now that sounds sexy, I can't wait to see him tomorrow. The way his name sounds makes my panties wet."

"Girl, you are crazy. See, I told you if you keep drinking that wine you're going to be drunk."

"Girl, please! I know how to handle my liquor. I'm going to call someone over to order us another bottle."

"Excusez-moi."

"Oui."

"Est-ce que vous parlez anglais?"

"Oui."

"Good, I thought that I would have to speak in French all night. Could we please have another bottle of your La boutelle devin?"

"Yes, you can. I'll be right back."

"Girl, he sounds sexy. I need to have me a little Frenchman tonight."

"Monica, you are tripping. When we finish this bottle we are heading back to the hotel so that we can get ready for tomorrow. If I keep you out all night you are going to be a mess in the morning, and I don't need for you to be looking half crazy during this photo shoot."

"GI-GI, I'm going to be okay, you need to make sure you are alright and that you're not the one looking crazy. 'I know how to handle my liquor,' yeah right," Monica said with a giggle. "I remember that time when we were in Miami and we went to that club. You drank the whole bottle of Patrón and I had to get someone to help me carry your behind out of there." GI-GI was laughing so hard she almost peed on herself.

"Yes, I do remember. I could not sleep my head was spinning so bad. I had to make myself vomit in order to finally go to sleep, and when I did the next day I was no good at all."

"I know because you could not get up, you couldn't even stand any noise. All you wanted to do was stay in the bed and drink water."

"Hell, I had to. I had a hot box stomach, I couldn't even eat anything. I promised myself that I would never get that way again—and I haven't."

"I'm glad because I'm not gonna be carrying your ass or trying to find someone to help me get your ass back to our room while we are here."

"Don't worry. I'm good." While the ladies continued their conversation, the waiter brought them another bottle of wine.

"Thank you."

"You're welcome."

"After we finish with this bottle we are going to go dancing, but we will not drink anything else unless it's some coffee."

"Look! You were the one telling me I need to get out of the attitude that I'm in, and now that I'm feeling good and relaxed you want to cut the drinking short?"

"You damn right, I need for you to be ready for work in the morning and looking appropriate, not like you just came out of the alley somewhere."

"Okay, okay, after we finish up here we can go dancing for a while and afterwards we can go in."

"Sounds good to me."

Once Monica and GI-GI finished their dinner and drinks, they decided to find a night club to go to and do a little dancing. Both ladies were feeling pretty good after the two bottles of La boutelle de vin. They proceeded to leave and find a hot spot to go to. They strolled to the exit of the restaurant, pushed open the door and stepped out into the cool night air. As they were leaving, the gorgeous man that they saw in the hallway of the hotel earlier was walking in.

"Bonsoir madame," the gorgeous man spoke. Both ladies looked at each other because they didn't know if he was talking to them or what.

Monica began to speak for them. "Are you talking to us?" she pointed her finger at herself before gesturing to GI-GI.

"Oui," the stranger smiled showing a full set of straight, startling white teeth.

"Well, do you speak English? Because right now we have a little buzz and we can't understand what you are saying." Monica giggled a little, as she glanced at GI-GI and covered her mouth with her hand to contain herself. She definitely didn't want to embarrass herself in front of this good looking stranger.

"I said, good evening ladies," the stranger spoke in a smooth voice with a sexy accent.

"Well, hello to you, too. I saw you in the hallway earlier, are you following us are something? You know how men are when they see nice looking women," Monica said, as she smoothed down her dress.

"No, I'm not following you. I eat here a lot, this is one of my favorite places, and I remember your beautiful face." Monica smiled at the comment that was directed at her. "So why are you two leaving so soon? You don't like the food?"

"The food was great and the wine was better, but we are headed out to find somewhere to dance."

"Okay, well make sure that you are careful out there. Two pretty ladies should have a man by their side."

"You have a pretty good game, but we'll be okay. You have a nice dinner; maybe we'll see you next time."

"I hope so." He flashed his smile again before turning and walking into the restaurant.

"Girl, were you flirting with that man?"

"No," Monica said, cocking her head to the side and looking at GI-GI out of the corner of her eye. "*He* was flirting with *me*. Talking about 'two pretty ladies like us need a man by our side,'" she said mocking the stranger's accent while rolling her neck. "I simply told him that we would be fine and to have a nice dinner."

"That was the guy that we saw in the hall early. And God, he is sexy and has the most beautiful set of lips—and those beautiful gray eyes. Ump, ump, ump…I hope I bump into him in the hotel again because if I do, I intend to find out who he is."

"Girl, you are a mess."

"Yes, I am, now with that let's go in here and have some fun." The ladies ended up at a club called "Cuckoo Club." When the ladies walked in they were in shock, because the layout of the club was so different from clubs back home in the States.

It was situated over two floors and the decor was just beautiful. The walls were a beautiful bright color, the music was reminiscence of the old days, and you could happily dance on the sofa. They also had a section where you could eat if you wanted, but the ladies decided not to only because they had already eaten and the prices were expensive. There was plenty of space and lots of celebrities were there.

"Girl, this place is magnificent. I never saw anything like this at home."

"It is magnificent, and check out all of the people in here enjoying the atmosphere."

"Well, let's do what we came here to do, and that is to hit the dance floor." The ladies danced all night. When they left it was around 2:00 a.m. and both ladies were exhausted.

"GI-GI, I didn't know we stayed in the club that long. Girl, we were having so much fun that time ran by us," Monica said.

GI-GI nodded in agreement. "Well, at least I can say I had a wonderful time." Once the ladies entered their hotel suite, they both headed to their rooms and fell asleep.

Shelia

Shelia closed the door after Marcus left, she was so tired that she went back up to her bedroom and went to sleep. It was around 2:30 when Shelia woke up and she looked at her phone and noticed that she did not have a missed call from Marcus. She also checked her cell, but nothing was there either. She felt bad, but then she remembered that he said he also needed some rest and had to do some work.

Well, let me take a bath and relax my body, Shelia thought as she was getting her bath together. She poured in some vanilla bath gel from Bath & Body Works and lit her vanilla scented candles. While taking off her gown she thought about Marcus. That man knows he can work that nine inch dick. It's funny but it's just right for my pussy, long and thick—pretty too, not a two-tone dick, but just one color "RED." Last night was great and I'm definitely going to see him again, not just for his body, but also for his company. He knows how to hold a woman's attention with conversation and all. We both were feeling each other. Just the thought of him gives my body chills. Damn, I forgot my cell phone, just in case he calls while I'm in here. This could be the beginning of a new relationship, I just have to make sure that I play my cards right. I don't want to be too aggressive and run him away, but I also don't want to sit back and make him think that I'm trying to be hard to get. Once I get out of the tub I'm going to give him a call.

Shelia began to bath her body all over. The candles were giving off an intoxicating scent and she was enjoying relaxing in her bath. She rubbed her body all over with the shower gel and made sure that she got every inch of her body. When she finished, she put warm water in her bottle and inserted it into her vagina to clean herself out. After she finished, she dried herself off and wrapped her towel around her. She went downstairs to make herself some tea, and then she headed back upstairs to her bedroom to put on some lounging clothes. She knew she wouldn't be going out. She wanted to take another nap, but she had to make a few calls to some clients that she had to show a house to tomorrow. Once she finished dressing she picked up her cell phone and headed back downstairs. It began to ring as she descended the stairs. She looked at the number and, of course, it was Marcus. Shelia's face lit up with a big smile.

Sharon/Henry

Sharon pulled up in her dad's driveway. As she was getting out she had to pull herself together. She was still a little nervous from running the red light and she did not want her dad to see the tension in her body. She put her key in the door to unlock it, but before she could turn the key her dad was already opening up the door for her.

"Hey baby girl, come on in."

"Hey dad, what are you up to in here? It smells good."

"I'm just cooking up some stuff for you and my grandchild."

"Here we go already. You are not going to spoil this child, okay? You are going to treat this grandchild just like you did me."

Her dad grinned. "You had it easy, baby girl."

"Please! Dad, no I didn't. I had it hard, but I thank you for it 'cause a lot of my classmates either ended up in jail, dead, pregnant or on drugs," Sharon said shaking her head.

"We did our best with you."

"You and mom did great with me. Where is Poochie?"

"I put her outside so she wouldn't be all over you."

"Dad, please. She doesn't need to be outside, she belongs indoors."

"Well, she is out there today. One thing about her, she will not get herself dirty. She is more like a human instead of a dog." After Sharon's mom passed her dad was so lonesome that he talked with Sharon about getting a dog. She told him that it would be nice to have a pet around. At least he would have some company in the house with him, so he went out and bought a silky Terrier. He decided to name her Poochie.

Henry was a tall dark man, with broad shoulders and graying hair. He had stern beady eyes. When he looked at you it would scare you because he could tell when you were lying or telling the truth. His voice was very deep and strong so when people met him for the first time it usually caught them off guard. Henry was a very strong man, and he took care of his family. He would make no mistakes about letting you know what he would do to you if you hurt one of his ladies. So when Sharon was gowning up, if a guy who liked her was brave enough to come to their house he would let them know straight off the consequences for hurting his daughter. "And don't try to hide because I will find you," he'd say to the young men. So there were not many guys that would mess with Sharon.

"Dad, I'm going to let Poochie in so I can play with her for a minute, if you don't mind."

"Go ahead, baby girl, this will give me a chance to finish up with dinner."

Sharon went to the back door and let the dog in. Once she came back in she ran right to Sharon's dad.

"Move girl, I'm trying to do something here."

"Look at her she is so pretty," Sharon said stroking her silky fur. "You are keeping her up good, dad."

"Yeah, and trust me, it costs to keep these dogs up and make sure that they are getting their shots and stuff."

"Look at her with that bow in her hair. You keep her up pretty good," she repeated again.

"She does look good, huh? I wish your mom was here to see me dealing with a dog," he laughed.

"Me too," Sharon replied. As Sharon played with Poochie she talked with her dad about her job, Monica and what was going on in her life right now. "Dad, how did I not know that Darryl was married? I should have been more cautious with him like I was with everyone else," Sharon said shaking her head. "I gave my all to that man and what has happened here is serious. There is a baby growing inside of me that did not ask to be here, and I cannot just act like it is okay. What am I suppose to tell my child? That I was sleeping with a married man?"

"No, you are going to tell your child the truth, what we have always taught you to do no matter what. You cannot go around here beating yourself up over this, you are a grown woman and no one can judge you. There is not a heaven or hell that *they* can put you in, once you talk with your God then that's all that matters. I know you are wondering what friends and family are going to say, but the hell with what they say. I got your back and you know that I'm not going to let anyone mess with my girl."

"I know, dad. Remember how you would scare the guys when I was in high school and they would be afraid to ask me out?"

"Yep. And if I have to start all over again, I would. So with that, are you ready to feed my grandchild some of this good food I have cooked up?"

"Yes, I 'm ready to try whatever you have in these pots."

Sharon had a plate full of food sitting in front of her. Her dad had cooked cabbage, baked chicken, fried chicken, fried corn, cornbread, black-eye peas and okra. He also placed a glass full of tea in front of her. "Dad, this is just too much. Why did you cook all of this food?"

"When my baby girl told me that she was coming over I wanted to make you the best meal ever," he said with a smile.

"Well you did, and I thank you."

Henry prepared himself a plate of food and they sat at the table and ate together. "Now, you know if you are not able to eat all of that you can take the rest home."

"I know, I planned on taking me some home anyway. This is going to be my lunch and dinner for two days. Plus, I'm eating just like the doctor told me, he said to eat good and not a lot of junk," Sharon said, placing a forkful of cabbage into her mouth.

"Well, I hate to say this, but you have a banana pudding waiting on you for desert."

"Dad, you didn't!"

"Yes, I did."

After they ate, they both cleaned the kitchen together. They were so full they retired to the den and watched the movie *Seven Pounds* together. Sharon fell asleep watching the movie. Her dad looked at her with so much admiration. He knew that Sharon was a good girl and would not try to get herself pregnant on purpose. He was going to do everything in his power while he was alive to make sure that she and this baby were just fine.

"I love you baby girl," he whispered. Henry continued to watch the movie while his daughter slept. He made sure that she was not disturbed, so when her cell phone rang he clicked the reject button on it.

Sharon woke up around 6:00 p.m. She looked for her father but did not see him. She got up from the couch where she was laying and called out to her dad. Once she did not see him in the house she begin to get nervous, but when she looked out of the door and saw her dad sitting on the porch she felt so much better.

"Hey dad, I'm about to head home. Is there anything you want me to do before I leave?"

"No. Look, I want you to promise me that while you are away from me that you will take care of yourself and do as the doctor ordered."

"I promise, dad." Sharon got into her car and headed towards home. She was feeling pretty good since she had spent some quality time with her dad. She smiled to herself and felt a warm feeling come over her. She always said that when she got that feeling it was her mom's way of telling her that everything is going to be okay. "Thank you, mom."

Once Sharon made it to her house and inside, she put her plate of food that she got from her dad into the refrigerator and went into her den. She felt her phone vibrate and looked at the number. It was Marcus. She wondered what he wanted with her, and she also saw that she had a miss called from him so Sharon decided to call him back to see what he wanted.

Darryl/Essie

Darryl left the house and drove over to his mom's. He wanted to tell her about the conversation he'd had with Sharon. But before Darryl got to his mother's he stopped at the store to buy some beer. He knew that his mom would say something about him drinking but wouldn't dwell on it long, so he decided to pick up a six pack before he got there. That way he would have time to drink about three before he got there. After exiting the store, Darryl got back into his truck and headed to his mom's house. He took the long way there so he could take his time and enjoy some of his beers. He believed in respecting his mother's wishes so he wouldn't drink around her. Darryl listened to Frankie Beverly's CD while he drunk his beer. His favorite song on there was "I Want to Thank You." Every time he heard that song he would think about Sharon because that's the song he would sing to her when she would be cooking dinner for them.

By the time Darryl pulled up to his mother's house he had just about finished the whole six pack of beer. He was enjoying the evening and he knew that his mom would have something good in the kitchen to eat. While walking to his mom house he though back on when he was a little boy staying in this neighborhood. It wasn't the best, but it wasn't the worst either. Darryl knew who to hang with and who not to hang with. There were certain places in his neighborhood that he was not allow to go, because that side was where they sold drugs, so him and some of the other kids would hang out in the street in front of their house playing basketball and chasing the girls. Darryl remembered being head over heels in love with Lisa who stayed across the street from them. He looked across the street over at the house that Lisa and her family once lived in and wondered how she was doing now. He hadn't seen her since her parents passed away.

Darryl unlocked the door and walked into his mom's house. He called out to her when he didn't see her in the kitchen. Darryl walked around the house looking for his mom and calling out to her. When he didn't get a response he began to panic. He knew that his mom was very particular about who she would let into her house, so this was unlike her. He looked around the house once again to see if anything was out of the normal. He also checked out the backyard trying to see if anything looked strange. By time Darryl walked back into the house heading towards the living room, just as he was about to pull out his cell phone and call the police, his mom walked through the door laughing with her friend Connie. They had just left church where they had been at a meeting.

"Mom, where in the world have you been? I came in here and didn't see you, and I got worried. I was just about to call the police," he said breathing a sigh of relief.

"Boy, what's wrong with your tone of voice? It's sounding pretty loud and I know you are not talking to me in that tone," his mom replied with a stern look.

"Sorry mom," Darryl mumbled dropping his head, "but I was worried about you."

"First of all, you need to speak and then apologize to me for that tone you have in your voice. If you must know, I left a message on your cell phone letting you know where I would be this evening if you just happened to come by, like you did. See, I knew you would be coming by that's why I made dinner for you and Marcus. Go on and take your smart-mouth behind in the kitchen and fix you something to eat while I finish talking with Connie." Essie and Connie both looked at Darryl and shook their heads as he sulked to the kitchen. Connie said her goodbyes and left Essie so that she could spend time with her son.

"So Darryl, how are things going with you and Tameka, the same or worse?"

"Worse, she is so full of it you would think that she has never done anything wrong, like she's a saint or something. I know it doesn't justify what I've done, but don't make me look like I'm the villain either."

"You and Tameka are going to have to find a way to get through this. You guys need to try and get some counseling before this turns ugly."

"Mom, I'm not trying to work things out with Tameka. It's over for me. Like I told you before, a lot has been going on in our marriage, this time it just took it out of the ballpark. There is no marriage left for us to fix. It's over!"

"So have you both made that decision? Are you sure this is what you want?" she paused for a moment. "You need to go and see your wife. Sit down and talk to her about all of this and see how she is really feeling about all of this. You are not in this marriage by yourself, so you just can't make this decision on your own. If this divorce was to happen between you two then you need to get control of yourself before Tameka makes it worse than it already is. Have you forgotten that you have a child on the way? So you need to be logical about this."

"I know mom, I'm just so angry right now. I messed up everything and I don't know where to start."

You need to start by talking with God and asking him to guide you. Ask him for forgiveness because the vows that you took in front of him you have broken them. You have to go to God, Darryl, so that he can help you. I told Tameka the same thing. I can't tell you what to do, the only thing that I can do is give you advice like I'm doing now. I'm sorry that all of this has happened, but only God knows our destiny so look to him, not to man."

"Thank you, mom, you are the best."

"I know," she replied. Darryl and his mom both started laughing after her statement. They ate and enjoyed each other's company. She told him about her meeting at church that they were trying to plan the church's anniversary.

Darryl told his mom all about Sharon, what type of work she does and what kind of person she is. He explained to his mom that she really didn't have any idea that he was married, and how sorry he was for destroying her life the way he has. He even told her about the dream he had with the little girl in it.

"Mom, I just cannot see myself not in this child's life. I love this baby already, I will not dare walk on this earth and not be a part of this child's life.

"I understand and I totally agree with you, but I want you to make sure that you get a chance to talk with Tameka and tell her everything. I know that it's going to be hard and a lot of good is not going to come out of this, but the sooner you do it the quicker it will be over with. Then you can decide what you and Sharon will do about the baby."

"I will, I promise. Well, I'm going to get going, I'll call you before the week is out to check on you, and the next time call the house if I don't answer my cell phone. I got scared when I didn't see you anywhere in here." Darryl wrote Marcus's home number down before he left out the door and headed to his truck.

Shelia/Marcus

"Hello."

"Hey pretty lady."

"Marcus?"

"Yes, who did you think it was? You waiting on someone else to call you?"

"No. I was beginning to think that you were lying."

"Now why would I do that when I had such a wonderful night with a beautiful woman like you?"

Sharon could not contain her smile she was so happy to be hearing from him. "You need to stop that, you got me blushing over here."

"That's what I want to do, keep you smiling so that you won't be trying to run off to someone else."

"Marcus, you need to stop."

"Stop what, telling you the truth? Look, I know that we didn't get to talk about a lot of stuff last night. We started, but other things happened that I didn't want to happen so soon, but it was our body chemistry I guess. But don't think for one minute that I did not enjoy every bit of it, because I did. I want to tell you everything there is about me, the good and the bad so that we can really know each other. The reason I want to do this is because

Shelia, I am Philogyny and I don't want to start off wrong with you. I have a problem with loving many women. So what do you say to dinner tomorrow night on me? We can go to a nice restaurant of my choice and I will show you how I do it."

"Okay, I would really like that." Shelia was outdone. She was not expecting this from Marcus. She thought that he would be calling her trying to talk that playboy talk, so she had prepared herself for the playgirl talk, but when he went to the left on her, it left her speechless.

"Hey pretty lady, are you still there? You got quite on me."

"Yeah, yeah, I'm here. So do I need to meet you or what?"

"No, I will be at your house to pick you up. Didn't I just tell you that I'm going to show you how I do it? Once you finish showing your last house call me and let me know what time to pick you up."

"Okay, so how should I dress?"

"I'll let you know about that tomorrow, but you don't have to go all out of the way. You are beautiful just the way you are."

"Well, thank you," Shelia replied with a smile.

Shelia and Marcus continued their conversation laughing and joking about different things. He told her how Darryl was trying to find out about what went on with them and that he was not about to tell him anything right now because he did not want to mess things up by talking too much. He told her how Darryl was his best friend and that they had been friends since they were kids. After about an hour and a half of talking, they let each other go. "Don't forget to call me when you finish with your last house," Marcus reminded.

"I won't. I can't wait to see how you do it," Shelia teased.

"Okay, pretty lady, you'll see. This will be a night that you won't forget, but I'm going to let you go and I will see you on tomorrow, okay?"

"Okay, I'm looking forward to it."

After Shelia hung up the phone she was smiling from ear-to-ear. She was excited about their date and had no idea what she was going to wear. She decided before she went in to work that she would go and buy something new for this date. If they end up as a couple then she definitely had to make herself look gorgeous on their first *real* date.

Tameka/Sadie

"Hi mom, I'm here," Tameka called as she walked into her mom's home.

"Hey baby, you ready to go? We can go to that new restaurant. They have the best soul food ever."

"That would be good, let's get going."

As Tameka and her mom Sadie headed out to the car, they discussed how good church was today. Once inside the car Sadie turned Tameka's radio to the gospel station. "Here I Am" by Marvin Sapp was playing. As they listened to the words, they both moved their heads from side to side.

"The words to this song are so powerful," said Sadie. "You can feel this song deep down in your soul if you are going through something. Tameka, I know that something is not right with you right now; I can feel it in my spirit. I know you baby, and I know that you wouldn't have been at church if something wasn't wrong. I have been asking you for over two years to come to church with me, but you always put it off. What is going on baby? You can talk to me. I know I haven't always been there for you, but I'm here now, so whatever it is, talk to me." They continued to drive in silence listening to the comforting words of the song before Sadie spoke up again. "When you get a chance, go get this song and let it minister to you."

"Mom, so much as happened in so little time. Darryl and I are not together anymore. I found out that Darryl has been cheating on me for a year. I knew something was wrong, but I couldn't put my hands on it. But it all came out this week."

"Did he admit this to you?"

"Yes, he did?"

"What in the world has gone on with you two? You were so happy together."

"We were happy at one time, but things have changed between us in the last couple of years. Darryl feels like I have been treating him like I'm his mother instead of his wife, we don't go anywhere together, let alone be intimate with each other."

"Well do you? And if you do, you need to stop so that you and this man can get back together," Sadie replied folding her arms across her chest and gazing out the passenger side window.

"Mom, there is no getting back together. Darryl has moved out. Well, I put him out after all of this. I couldn't take it any longer. He told me he doesn't love me anymore. So much has been said that I really don't think I want him back. Just the thought of him sleeping with someone else makes me sick to my stomach," Tameka said with a frown as she glanced over at her mom.

"I need to talk to him."

"NO! Mom, I don't want you saying anything to him about this. This is something that I have to handle on my own, and I will. When all of this is over with I will have survived and God has something else in store for me. I don't know what it is right now, but I know that I'm going to make it. Like I told Pastor today, that message was for me, God has a way of doing things and I'm going to walk in his will from now on—not mine."

"Well, baby, all I can do is respect your wishes. I'm going to be here for you, just remember that." By the time they arrived at the restaurant they were both ready to eat. Once they were seated at their table, they already knew what they wanted to order. When the waiter came over, both ladies placed their orders and talked some more about Tameka's situation.

"Tameka, I want you to know that whatever you decide and whatever you do, you are not in this alone. If you want to come and stay with me until all of this plays out, then come home."

"Mom, I'm not going to come home. Out of all of this I will not allow Darryl to run me away from my house. He is the one that went out and cheated on me, if I don't get anything else out of this, I will get to keep my house."

"Well, I don't blame you for that."

The waiter came back with their food, and both ladies started digging in. "This food is really good, mom."

"I told you, Mable has some good food here. Me and some of the ladies comes here after church every other Sunday."

"I'm glad that you're able to still have a good time with your friends and not let life consume you with the troubles of this world."

"Baby, you live long enough and you will see how easy it is to not let stuff get to you anymore. God has a way of doing things, sometime we can move and do things on our own and it's not what he had planned for us. I know the way things went about with you and

Darryl when you all first meet, but if you think about it, that was a move you and Darryl made, not God. See Tameka, God already has our life planned out for us, but we want to go and do our own thing so he allows us to do it, but he also helps us out of it so that we can do it right the next time. Now the next time—if it may be a next time, let God send you the man that he wants you to have." She paused to take a bite of her food before continuing. "The reason that I can tell you this is because I thought that your father was the man for me, but he wasn't. The things that I went through with him were entirely too much. I thought that I could change him from drinking every weekend and fooling around with all types of women, but one day I came to my senses. That's when I packed up our things and left. I prayed to God for a man that truly loves the Lord and would love his wife like God loved the church, a man that was honest and was God-fearing. I prayed just about every night and one day that's when Carl came along. I was working at the cleaners trying to make it for us. He would come in every Wednesday to pick up his clothes and drop off the one's he wanted cleaned. He would try to talk to me. At first, I would not pay him any attention, but one day he pleaded with me to go out with him. I asked one of my co-workers that I had become close to, to keep you and she did. I went out and had a wonderful time that night. After that, we started dating for about two years before we got married. That was the best thing that ever happened to me besides you. I loved your father, but I was *in love* with Carl. He treated me with so much respect and he took to you as if you were his own."

"He was a good step-father. I can remember when he took me to my first NBA basketball game. I think I had more fun at the game than he did. He made sure that wherever I had to be, he would be right there if he didn't have to work. He was more like a father to me than a step-father. I was grateful to have a man like dad in my life, and on that tragic day when he departed from us to go be with God, I thought that neither one of us would ever recover from that."

"God has really brought us through. It was really hard for me, baby. You just don't know. Some nights I would stay up all night long just waiting on him to walk through the door, and when I finally realized that he was gone for good, I would sit up and cry half of the night. My friends could tell how bad I was grieving, they would pray over me every day. I can remember one day I was in the kitchen washing dishing and God spoke to my spirit. He told me to stop questioning him about why this happened, and just know that he does all things for a reason. He told me regardless of how things looks he would bring me out, and to stop crying because your father was at peace, and he was happy. After God spoke to me, I sat down at the table and I prayed with a purpose. A purpose to remove the sadness from me and to let me get my joy back and live my life until the day that I could be reunited with Carl. And I can tell you ever since then, I have been happy," Sadie said with a smile. "So what I'm trying to tell you is that one day God will send you that man that he wants for you, you just hold on to his unchanging hands. All this is for a reason, but we just don't know what that reason is. I thank God for each and every day that I had with Carl. He gave me a man that was full of love and life, a man that loved the Lord. Just like it came to me, you will get it. And if you don't, don't worry about it, you got God and that's the only thing that really matters."

"Mom, you make it sound so good."

"It is. You just have to believe it for yourself. Like I told you, it's not going to be easy but keep praying, and reading the word. Everything that you need is in the book. You get that Bible, start reading it for yourself and give God what is due to him, and in the mist of the storm, he will give you Peace."

"I will. I love you mom, just hearing you tell me all of this makes it better. I just got to get myself together to talk with Darryl and talk to him without any hate, because I don't want to feel that way towards him, so I got a lot of praying that I need to do. I have to be able to forgive him and move on with my life so that God will be able to bless me. Sometimes, I really believe that it's because I can't have any kids that our marriage was rocky too."

"Darryl knew this before he married you. You told him that you couldn't have kids, he didn't have a problem with it then, and if he did, this is really selfish of him. Baby, all I'm going to do is pray for you. You will get through this and come out even stronger."

After the ladies finished their dinner they left the restaurant and headed back to Sadie's house. They drove in silence listening to the gospel station again. This time Mary, Mary's "Yesterday" was playing. They both listened to the song without any comments because they knew what the other was thinking. Once they pulled up to Sadie's house, Tameka got out of the car and walked her mom to the house. She went inside the house with her to make sure that she was okay before she left for the day.

"Well, Mom, I have enjoyed this day. I will call you before the week is out."

"You do that, keep me informed on what is going on, and if you need to come over and stay for a couple of days you have your key. Know that I love you and I'm here for you. I'm in this with you, you are not alone so don't walk around here with you head hanging down. You keep your head up and stay STRONG."

"I will, I love you and I'll talk with you before the week is out." Tameka left out of her mom's house with a feeling of love. She knew that sometimes her and her mom could be at odds with each other, but one thing she knew for sure was that her mom PROTECTS her family, that was what she really loved about her. So she didn't have to worry about anything because her mom had her back. Once Tameka made it home she got herself ready for bed. She took a shower and afterwards, she made herself a cup of coffee, got out her Bible and started praying asking God to give her a word. She opened her Bible to 2nd Chronicle, chapter 20, verse 17. *Ye shall not (need) to fight in this (battle): set yourselves, stand ye (still), and see the salvation of the LORD with you, O Judah and Jerusalem: fear not, nor e dismayed; tomorrow go out against them: for the LORD (will be) with you.* After reading this she was filled with peace. She knew that she had God on her side and she was going to let him fight her battles.

Monica

Oh God......my head is hurting so bad, that wine from last night has really put a hammer on me. I will not be drinking that anymore while I'm here, I'm just gonna stick to my beer. God, what time is it? When Monica looked at the clock on the nightstand she only had an hour to get ready to go to the studio for her shooting. *Let me get in here and get a shower, I really do need some coffee and something on my stomach before I be sick all day,* she thought, as she rummaged through her purse for a bottle of aspirin.

Monica went into the bathroom and took a shower. After about fifteen minutes she forced herself to get out, any longer and she would really be late. Once she got out of the shower and lotioned herself up, she threw on some jeans and a t-shirt. Once she arrived on set the stylists would be dressing her for her photo shoots anyway. Instead of coffee, she grabbed herself a cup of orange juice, then she called to see if the driver was downstairs ready. After she hung up the phone she grabbed a bagel and headed out of the suite. *I see GI-GI is already gone, she must have order all of this when she got up. She knew I was in bad shape,* she thought as she stepped out of the suite and proceeded to the elevator. My girl warned me last night about that wine, but I wouldn't listen. She does look out for me; that's why I love her, even though sometimes she can get on my last nerve. While driving to the studio Monica was looking out of the window at all of the glamorous buildings and statues on the street. When they pulled up at the studio, the driver got out and opened the rear door and helped Monica out of the limo. Just as she was getting out and walking towards the studio, the first person she saw was the handsome man from the restaurant.

"Oh my God, what in the world is he doing here? I hope he is not one of the photographers; this is really going to be difficult for me. On top of that, I have a hangover from hell. This is not good, not good at all," Monica mumbled under her breath. She searched for GI-GI so she could find out what was going on with the handsome guy. Monica asked around to some of the staff to see if they knew where she was, but no one had seen her. By the time Monica was heading back to the front of the building, GI-GI was coming out of the restroom.

"GI-GI, what's that guy doing here? You know the handsome man. I hope he is not doing the photo shoots because I look a hot-ass mess from last night. All I want to do is get started and get this over with. I have the worst headache," Monica said, massaging her temples with both her hands.

"I'll just bet you do. I told you last night to slow down on the drinking, but Mrs. Thing would not listen to me. First, let me go get you something for your headache and then I'll explain everything to you about Mr. Handsome."

"Please do. This has to be a mistake," Monica replied with a sigh.

GI-GI left to go and get something for Monica's headache, while she was gone that's when Mr. Laird came over and spoke with Monica.

"Hi Monica, how are you this morning? Did you ladies have a good time last night? You know the clubs here can really put a toll on you if you keep at it all night," he said with a smile. While he was talking to Monica he was laughing inside because he knew that she was not feeling well. He could see it written all over her face. She had, had a little too much to drink last night and he was going to make sure that they did not have to do a shoot tomorrow. That way she could get some rest after she left the set. But he was not about to let her go without setting up a date. There was something about her that he liked, that's why when he saw her pictures he found out what agency she worked for and made it his business to get her to come to Paris and do this job. He was determined to get to know her before she flew back to the States. He wanted her, and he always got what he wanted.

When GI-GI returned she saw the two talking and she wondered what was going on this time. She rushed over to them because she didn't want Monica to do or say anything crazy to this man. He was the *boss* and was paying good money.

"I got your aspirin, girl," she said handing Monica two aspirin and a bottle of water. "Look, we need to get you on back so that you can get ready to work. Mr. Laird is there anything you need from Monica before we head out? We don't want to be late for work," GI-GI said giving him her best smile.

"Oh, wait a minute…there is one thing that I would like to request from her."

Monica looked crazy and wondered what this man was about to say, and GI-GI was wondering what had been said before she got back to them. She was just as shocked as Monica when she heard his request.

"Monica, it would bring me great pleasure if you would go out on a date with me," he said looking her straight in the eyes.

Monica dropped her head to break the spell of his mesmerizing gaze. "Mr. Laird, I don't think I can do that, I don't know you and I'm here to work," she stammered.

"You will work and I will make sure that I don't keep you out late. I wouldn't want the boss to get upset with you," he said with another smile. He was having too much fun watching Monica squirm.

"I can't do that," Monica said twisting her hands together. Just being near this gorgeous man was causing her to feel jittery.

"Sure you can, all you have to do is say yes, and I will handle the rest."

"Look, I really have to get to work."

"Well, I'll be here, so when you finish we can finish this conversation about our date."

As Monica walked away she asked GI-GI again why was this man here. "All I want to do is get this started so that I can get back to the room and get in bed."

"Umm huh. You'll listen to me next time, won't you?" GI-GI said with a light chuckle. She stopped walking and placed her hand on Monica's arm to stop her too. "Listen, Monica, I need to tell you this before you hear it from other people. Mr. Laird is our boss." GI-GI paused for a moment to let her words sink in. "Mr. Too-Fine back there is the one that wanted you to model his clothing line. He saw your work and liked it. I didn't know it was him until I got here this morning. I was just as surprise as you were, but we got to be on our best behavior with this one. He is paying good money and we don't want to lose him just in case he wants to use us again."

Monica stood briefly with her mouth hanging open. "You mean to tell me that *he* is our boss?" she said dumbfounded.

"Yes, and he knew who we were but we didn't know him."

"Okay," Monica said rubbing her chin as she thought. "I can handle this one, he thinks he's slick, but I got something for him."

"And what exactly is that, Monica? Don't do anything stupid, this is your career we're talking. Hell, mine too!"

"I'm not. The only thing I hate about it is that he's our boss and I really like him. I just get nervous when he comes around."

Monica worked for several hours before they called it quits. She was so exhausted that all she wanted to do was take a long hot bath and go right to bed. But to her surprise when she was walking out of the building there he was waiting on her like he said he would be.

"You though I was gone? I told you I would be here when you finished. So what about that date?"

You know what? I will gladly take you up on that offer," she said with a smile. *What could it hurt?* she thought.

"So when would you like to go?"

"Not tonight. I'm very tired, and I'm afraid I wouldn't be good company."

"Tomorrow then?"

"Sure." Monica was shocked to say that she did accept Mr. Laird's invitation to dinner for the next day.

She didn't know what she was thinking or planning on doing since he tried to be slick with her. She didn't know if it was the hangover or the stress of being just plain exhausted from a hard day's work. Even though she was excited about it, she was still nervous at the same time. She decided to call her best friend and let her know what was going on, and besides, she wanted to check up on things back home.

Monica/Sharon

"Hello."

"Hey girl, what's going on with you? Besides getting ready to have a baby for us and eating on everything that you see," she laughed.

"Who say's I'm eating everything? Only ice cream, Butter Pecan."

"Well, I tell you what, when I get back home we are going to have a girl's night out at my house and we'll eat all different flavors of ice cream, me you, GI-GI and Kimberly. We are going to do it up for you and by the way, don't worry yourself with the baby shower, I'm going to handle that."

"Monica, I don't need a baby shower. You know that I don't deal with a lot of people and plus baby shower are for people who are married. You know I've always told you that if someone I know is having a baby and is not married, I don't go. That's just my prerogative."

"Go on with your bad self Bobby Brown, talking about 'it's your prerogative.'" Both ladies started laughing at what Sharon had just said. They talked for a while before Monica started telling Sharon how her day had gone and about her proposal for a date. "Well, I've been asked out on a date."

"And what did you say."

"I said yes."

"That's good."

"It's kinda good *and* bad. The company I'm here doing the shoot for, well, the guy who owns it asked me out. Sharon this man is gorgeous. When I say FINE! I mean *FINE!* It's funny because when GI-GI and I first got here we saw him getting on the elevators and we were talking about how sexy he was."

"So you all didn't know this was the man you were working for?"

"Nope. We had no idea. So we went and had dinner and just as we were leaving the restaurant, he walked in."

"Mr. Gorgeous?"

"Yes. We introduced ourselves, but all the while this man knew who we were. We had no clue that this was the man we would be working for. So when I got to work this morning once again this gorgeous man was there. I was starting to wonder if he was following us or something. I went searching for GI-GI to see why he was here. He came up to me talking as if we really knew each other, and before I left to go to wardrobe, he asked me out. Both me and GI-GI was looking real crazy."

"So what happened? You told him no?"

"I told him not tonight because I was exhausted, but he asked for tomorrow and I said yes, to my surprise. I don't know if it's the hangover or just tired. I just know that I don't want to mess up my job by going out with him. You know I take my job seriously and when you get involved with co-workers or bosses then that's when the worst begins to happen. It's funny how this job came about, because you know GI-GI usually knows the person that requests me."

"I know, plus it was all of a sudden and she had no clue who it was when I asked her."

"Monica, I can bet you that this man has been watching you. I'm talking about your work, and he likes what he sees, but trust me, it's not just your work it's also you. I would go out with him, have some fun, girl. At least one of us can do that."

"Sharon, I'm sorry for throwing all of this on you and you have a lot going on yourself that is more important. This is not like I'm about to make some life or death decision."

"Girl, please! We are best friends and that's what I'm here for—important or not. You know I talked with Darryl and it was good, but I don't know if I can ever give my all to him anymore. I also talked with my dad and he is thrilled about this baby. I had to realize that God's plans are not ours and he does things for a reason. I don't know what his reason is for this, but I'm going to stand strong and hold on to my faith. I got to trust God on this."

"I'm not going to argue with you on that, he sure does because my plan was to go and see my mom for a while, you know, give my brother a break. We need to get some stuff resolved. Life is too short and I don't want anything to happen to either one of us without having a mother and daughter relationship."

"I understand."

Monica and Sharon talked some more before they called it an evening. They told each other that they would keep in touch and to be safe. Sharon promised that she would get over to Monica's house and check on her mail after they each said I love you and hung up.

Darryl

Darryl was at work sitting at his desk, he was wondering if he should call Sharon and see when they could talk or let her call him. He was wondering how her and the baby was doing. Darryl wanted so badly to pick up that phone and call, but he didn't want to rush her with things. He wanted her to come to him on her own, because he felt if he kept calling her she would back away from him. He thought about her a lot, he knew that she was beautiful being pregnant and he just wanted to be with her at this time. *How foolish was I to do something so stupid to someone so special?* he thought. *God help me to do the right thing.* Darryl remembered what his mother told him, that he would have to go to God and pray. With his office door shut and locked, Darryl got down on his knees and prayed to God.

Heavenly Father, I come to you right now with a heavy load. I have sinned in your eye sight and I ask that you forgive me. Father I don't know how to pray, but I do know that you will hear me when I pray. I ask that you will guide me to do the right thing with this situation; you know what's going on right now. Lord, lead me in the right direction, I know that a baby has come out of this mess, but Lord you do not make mistakes. I ask that you protect this baby from any harm, allow me to be the best father that I can be, and Lord, please forgive me. If this marriage is meant to be with Tameka then you let your "Will" be done. Give me peace and let me be able to walk the way that you will have me to do in your precious son Jesus Name Amen.

Once Darryl finished praying he got up off of his knees and said, "Thank You, Jesus." He heard a knock on his door and when he opened it, to his surprise Tameka was standing there.

Tameka

Tameka stood at Darryl's office door with a look of peace on her face. She didn't know what to expect but she knew that she had to speak with him today. She wanted to let him know that out of all of this she was going to stand strong and not let this break her, that she would handle this with dignity. After reading her Bible last night she knew that God was with her every step of the way.

"Hi, Tameka."

"Hi, Darryl. Sorry for not calling, but I wanted to speak with you and I just took a chance on coming over here. Do you have time to talk? I can come back later if this is a bad time."

"Oh no, come on in and have a seat. Tameka, I just want to say I'm so..."

"Stop. I came here so let me do the talking. Darryl, I know that I was hard on you sometimes. There were some things that I said that I shouldn't have said and done. I was not the kind of wife to you that I could have been and I want to say that I'm sorry for that. When I slept with Gary and left you for those months you could have told everyone, but you didn't. I took you and our marriage for granted. All you were trying to do was work hard and make a home for us, but that wasn't enough for me so I went out and cheated on you. I never did say to you how sorry I was. I was only happy that you let me come back home when Gary ended up leaving me. No, I'm not happy about how things have turned out with us, but I was wrong for how I have handled this. I want you to know that I'm sorry for everything I have ever done to you and I came here hoping that you would forgive me."

"Tameka, I forgave..."

Tameka interrupted, "Let me finish while I can. I have been talking to someone who I know will help me through this." Darryl was looking at Tameka with a look of confusion, he was wondering if she had been talking with a male friend or a lawyer. He wanted to ask, but he just let her continue to talk. "I know you are probably wondering who this person is that I have been talking with."

Darryl was kind of relieved when she said that, but he didn't know why. *Yes GOD!* he thought to himself.

"I'm here because I want peace between us. I don't know if I can stay in this relationship, too much has happened and been said that can't be taken back. I don't want anything from you but to stay in the house. We were not put together by God, we did this on our own. We might pray and ask God to help us, but in the back of our minds we will not be able to trust each other. I have to let go so that I can find myself. I can't love you or anyone else until I learn how to love myself. So with all of this said, I'm going to let you get back to work. I can only wish that you have a great life. When you get ready to come by and get the rest of your things just let me know, I will try not to be there. It still hurts. I will not act like it doesn't, so I won't be there. I will also get with my lawyer and you can get with yours so that we can try to work out everything."

Darryl just stared at Tameka because he hadn't seen this side of her in years. He was wondering what had become of her. He knew that he needed to be honest with her like she was with him, but he just didn't know how. He was afraid of the consequences so he let her leave without saying anything about the baby. He kept saying to himself, *this is not the time.*

Darryl

After Tameka left Darryl shut the door behind her and stood in the same place praying to God. *Lord, I ask that you give me the courage to tell this woman the truth. Lord, you are the only person that can help me through this. I don't know how to tell this woman the truth. I have failed her in our marriage, but I just don't want to add more hurt to her. Give her the heart to be able to accept this when I tell her, help me to become the person that she has become. I ask you father to give both of us strength to be able to endure what lies ahead of us, in your son Jesus Name Amen.*

After Darryl finished praying he returned to his desk and laid his head back in his chair.

Shelia/Marcus

After Shelia finished with her last client she climbed back into her car and beginning dialing Marcus's cell phone number. She was excited about their date tonight. She was in a great mood all night after she had finished taking with him about today. Shelia called Marcus but he didn't answer his phone, so Shelia tried again. She knew that he should have been off of work by now so her mind went to wondering all kinds of things. She said to herself, "I knew it was too good to be tr—"

Before she could finish her sentence Marcus was calling her phone.

"Hello."

"Hey pretty lady, I'm sorry that I missed your call, I was in the store picking up some things. But I'm glad that you called. Dress casual tonight, it's going to be a romantic night, but you don't have to go all out of the way. I will be by to pick you up around seven o'clock so be ready."

"I will, see you soon." Once Shelia hung up from Marcus she only had three hours to get herself together. She knew if she ventured inside the mall she would be there all night. It was never her style to go into anywhere shopping and come right back out. Oh, no. It would take her at least three hours, so the mall was definitely out of the question. She would have to go home and look through her closet and pull out something. She had a couple of outfits in her closet that she hadn't worn so she would be okay for now, but the next time she would make it her business to go to the mall.

Shelia pulled up to her house and got out of the car. She was walking so fast that she didn't see the guy coming up behind her.

"Hey lady, give me your purse and don't turn around. If you do, I won't hesitate to put a bullet in your ass."

"Please don't hurt me. Take the purse, just let me go into my house safely. I promise I will not look back, just don't hurt me," Shelia spoke with terror in her voice.

"Shut up! I will do all the talking. Now, since you are running your damn mouth I want you to walk up to your door slowly. I will give you your keys once you get to the door, and don't try any funny shit, or I won't hesitate to kill you. Do you understand me?"

"Yes." Shelia walked slowly to her house with tears running down her face. She was so nervous, her legs were shaking so badly she was about to fall. But she knew that she had to hold herself up so no harm would come to her. She prayed all the way to the door asking God to protect her and keep her safe from all harm and danger. Once they got to the door he gave her the keys, grabbed her purse, and told her to stand there and count to fifty before she went inside. Little did he know, an undercover cop stayed right across the street from Shelia and was watching the entire incident. He turned and took off running, but to his surprise, he ran dead slap into Officer Taylor. Officer Taylor grabbed him off the ground and threw him against the car. Shelia heard the noise and turned around and saw what was going on. Officer Taylor hollered over to Shelia and told her to call 911. Once she did she also called Marcus.

"Hey pretty lady, are you ready already? I just knew it would take you forever."

"No, I'm not. I was calling to see if you could come right over. This guy just tried to rob me right in my own damn yard. He tried to run off with my purse, but by the grace of God, Officer Taylor was watching and took control of it," she stated breathlessly, trying to control her rapidly beating heart.

"Where is he now?" Marcus asked in disbelief.

"Officer Taylor has him now, I called the police and then you, but Marcus I'm scared. Could you please hurry over?"

"I'm on my way baby, just go in the house until the police arrive."

"I will." Shelia told Officer Taylor what she was about to do and asked did he need her to stay out there with him until help arrived.

"Yes, it would be good if you do because the officers are going to want to ask you some questions." While Officer Taylor held the robber down he asked Shelia if she was she okay and if she had anyone who could stay with her tonight.

"Yes, my friend is on his way." By the time she finished telling Officer Taylor that she would be okay they heard the siren and saw the police car coming towards them. Behind the police car was Marcus's truck. She was so relieved when she saw both vehicles that she didn't know what to do. Marcus jumped out of his truck and ran towards Shelia.

"Hey pretty lady, are you okay?" he asked taking her in his arms. "Did that bastard hurt you in any kind of way? If I could, I would go over there and kick his ass myself."

"I'm okay, just shaken up. Marcus, I don't know where he came from, all I know is that he was behind me. I was so afraid I just did what he asked me to do."

"It's okay, I'm here now and I'm not going anywhere. You are coming home with me tonight."

"Marcus, I can't..."

"Don't say a word, lady. Like I said, you are coming home with me."

While Shelia and Marcus talked, the police were taking a statement from Officer Taylor, and getting the details about what happened. One of the officers came over to Shelia to take her statement and to check and see if she was alright.

"Ms. Harris, I'm Officer Carmichael. How are you doing?"

"I'm okay, just shaken up some, it all happened so fast."

"I'm going to need to get a statement from you about what happened here tonight. Are you able to tell me what went on here?"

"Yes, I can do that, but could I please go inside of my house?"

"Sure."

As Shelia and Marcus proceeded to her house Officer Carmichael follow behind ready to take Shelia's statement while the other officer stayed outside with the robber and Officer Taylor.

"So could you tell me what exactly happened here tonight?"

"Yes, I was getting out of my car walking up to my house and from out of nowhere, he came from behind. I asked him not to hurt me, just take what he wanted and let me go. He told me to shut up and listen to him."

"What else did he say to you?"

"He told me to give him my purse. He said to walk to my house slowly and if I tried anything that he would not hesitate to kill me. I was so afraid that I did just what he told me to do. All I could do was pray to God for my safety. All I can remember is once we got to the door he gave me my keys and told me to start counting. I began to count, but then I heard a loud noise and I was afraid. I turned around, and that's when I saw Officer Taylor on him. I was so happy I put the keys in my lock, opened the door, and did what Officer Taylor told me to do."

"Do you know this guy? Have you ever seen him before today? Has anything strange been happening around here lately?" he asked, glancing around the room.

"Not that I know of, and it's pretty quite in my neighborhood. We have never had anything like this to happen. Why would he do something like this? I don't mess with anyone, why would someone want to rob me?"

"Calm down, baby. You are going to be all right, I'm not going to let anything happen to you."

"Well, we are going to take him to the station and book him, but I'm going to need for you to come down there."

"For what? I just told you everything that happened. I don't have anything else to say."

"We are just going to need a little more information and then we will let you go."

"What about him? Will he be in for a while?"

"He won't be going anywhere tonight so don't you worry about that."

"She won't have to worry because I will be with her. Look, Shelia, let's just go down to the station, answer the few question that they have for you, so that you can get back and get some rest. Like I told you earlier you will not be staying here tonight. You are going to stay with me so go and get you a bag together while I finish talking with Officer Carmichael."

Shelia went upstairs to retrieve a bag and some clothes. She was so tired all she wanted to do was get a shower and go to sleep. She really wouldn't get any rest because this would be her first time visiting Marcus's house and staying all night and she didn't know what to expect. But she didn't want to stay here at her house. Once Shelia finished getting everything that she needed, she went back downstairs to let them know that she was ready to go.

"Okay, I'm ready. I have everything I need for tonight."

"Don't worry about your car, leave it here. You are riding with me."

"Okay."

Once Shelia locked up her house and got in the vehicle with Marcus they followed the police car down to the station so that she could finish with the report. Once they all arrived at the station she told them once again what happened, then they left and headed towards Marcus's house.

"Marcus, I'm sooooo sorry about all of this, we had a date tonight and it has been ruined. You have gone through a lot just to show me a good time tonight and look at what happened."

"Shelia, I don't care about all of that as long as you are alright, that's the only thing that matters to me. Girl, I care about you and as long as we are together I'm not going to let anything happen to you. There was so much that I was going to tell you tonight about me and I still plan on doing so. We still have a date, it may not be the one that I had planned, but that's okay as long as we are still together. I'm going to enjoy this date so much better than the original one I planned," he said with a grin. Marcus was looking at Shelia with lust in his eyes and she saw it because she had that same look in hers.

"You are a mess, I know just what you were thinking," she said, smiling for the first time since all this had happened.

"And how do you know that? I didn't say anything out of the way," Marcus said with a raised eyebrow.

"You didn't have to say it. I saw it in your eyes, and don't try to deny it." They both started laughing as they continue to head towards Marcus's house. When they arrived they went inside and he showed Shelia where she could put her stuff. Marcus gave her a tour of his house and when he finished showing her around he took her to his master bathroom where she could take a shower. Then he went back downstairs to prepare them something to eat. But when he looked in the cabinet and refrigerator and couldn't find anything to put together quickly, he made a call for a pizza.

Darryl/Essie

Darryl called his mom to tell her what had just happened between Tameka and him, how she came to his office to let him know how she felt about everything. "Mom, I don't know how to tell Tameka the truth about Sharon. Once she left I prayed to God on what to do, but I'm still not sure. This woman told me how sorry she was about everything and that she forgives me for the way she acted. I'm afraid if I tell her the truth that it will really destroy her and she will really hate me for what I have done to her."

"Darryl, what do you expect? Do you really think that she is just going to accept that and not feel some kind of anger knowing that she could never have children by you?" She is going to be devastated and I don't know if she will ever forgive you or not, but you are going to have to tell her the truth, one way or the other. I have told you before that you have to seek God on this and ask him for your direction. Maybe that's what Tameka has done and was able to come and talk with you with an open heart. It's time for you to do the right thing by her because as long as you keep this in, you are not going to have peace."

"Mom, I have prayed to God. Right after she left I prayed. I just don't know what else to do. I want this to be done, but I'm afraid of what the consequences might be."

"Then you should have thought about this before you went out and cheated on your wife."

Darryl just held his head down when his mom made that statement. He knew that she was right, but he did not need for her to throw it in his face at a time like this. He knew that it was time for him to tell his mom what had happen between him and Tameka years ago.

"Mom, there's something I have to tell you about Tameka. But I don't want for you to see her any differently just because I'm telling you this. I just need for you to listen to me. Mom, Tameka cheated on me years ago."

"What? And you're just saying something about this?"

"Yes, when this happened I didn't tell anyone because I was ashamed of what had happened. Not only did she cheat on me, but she also moved out and moved in with the man that she was sleeping with. I know this might be the wrong time to bring it up but I'm not the only one in this marriage that has been unfaithful. Tameka stayed gone for a while and all that time I acted just like everything was fine. But one day she called me and asked if she could come back home because this man ended up leaving her. So yes, I took her back and continued to act just like it never happened. I didn't even bring it up to her after that. I just took her back because she was my wife, and at the time I was missing her."

"Darryl, right then you both should have gone to a marriage counselor so that things could have been fixed and maybe you both would not be where you are today."

"You're right, but we both have come to an understanding that this was not put together by God and that we need to go on with our separate lives. I still don't want to hurt her by letting her know about the baby. I know that sooner or later I'm going to have to tell her, maybe it's because she still has a part of my heart. I just can't erase her like that, we had some years together."

"Well, at least you know that, and that you still have her best interest at heart. I know that you still love her but if she was willing to tell you the truth then you should be willing to give her the truth, and I think that you need to do this soon."

"I know, I know, I'm going to call her up before the week is out and see if she will talk with me. I really appreciate you listening to me and I will let you know how everything turns out, but please send a prayer up for me. I think that he would listen to you before he listens to a sinner like me."

"Baby, God hears all of our prayers. We all have *sinned* and fallen *short* of his *word*. You go to God with this and ask him to give you the right words to say to her, and while you are praying, I will be praying too."

After Darryl hung up from his mom he decided to leave his office for a while because he couldn't get any work done. He had too much going on in his head. He decided that he would go to the mall and walk around maybe that would help him clear his mind.

Sharon

As Sharon was getting ready for her doctor's appointment she was a little nervous and excited. She was excited about having her first ultrasound done. She didn't tell anyone about this appointment but her dad. She wanted him to know everything that was going on with her and the baby because he was just as excited as she was. If she had told Monica she knew that she would try to make her find out the sex of the baby. She wanted so badly for Darryl to be with her, but she was still a little upset with him. This was something that they were supposed to be celebrating together. She began to wonder what he was doing. Once Sharon got herself together and finished doing everything that needed to be done she headed out the door to her vehicle and headed to the doctor's office. Sharon drove in silence thinking about her mom and how happy she would be right about now. When she reached her doctor's office her heart was beating so fast from excitement that she thought she was about to have a heart attack. When she walked in the office she signed her name on the clipboard and took a seat. Sharon was called back after she waited for about thirty minutes. The nurse took her through her normal routine checking her weight and height, getting urine from her and taking blood, followed by some questions about how she has been doing and if she was still taking her prenatal vitamins. By the time she finished with all of that, they lead Sharon back to another empty room with different types of equipment.

"Sharon I'm going to need for you to pull your pants down below your stomach and you can lift up your blouse. Now this gel that I'm about to apply to your stomach is going to be cold at first. As I examine you I will be explaining to you what I see and what is going on. You will hear your baby's heartbeat through the machine. We try to do that so that the parents will be more relaxed knowing that they can hear the baby's heart."

"Okay," Sharon nodded.

The nurse put the gel on Sharon's belly once she was laid back on the bed. She rolled the stick over her belly explaining the procedure. Sharon did become more relaxed when she heard her baby's heartbeat. While Sharon was laying there tears rolled down her face because all she could think about at that moment was having her family by her side—even Darryl. When the nurse saw the sad look on her face she gave her some tissue and asked her if she wanted to know the sex of her baby. At first she did, but after she thought about it, she changed her mind.

"No, I don't want to know, all I want to know is if the baby is doing okay."

By the looks of everything Sharon, your baby is doing great. All I can say is enjoy the rest of these few months and make sure to keep doing what you're doing. Okay,

I'm done here, let me get a towel to wipe you up and you are good to go." When the nurse finished up, she and Sharon walked out of the room together.

"Do I need to see the doctor before I leave?"

"No, you didn't have to see him for this visit, but you will spend some time with him on your next appointment. Sharon paid her co-pay to the young lady at the desk, got her appointment card, said thank you and left. While walking to her vehicle she was thinking about what she would treat herself to today. But first she had to get over to Max's house to check on Diamond, and then go by Monica's house. Sharon got into her vehicle and headed toward 65 going north. She listened to her CD while driving and thought to herself that she would treat herself to an outfit after she finish with this.

Sharon began to pray while she was driving. *God, I ask you right now in your son Jesus name that you help me raise this baby to have an anointing over his or her life. I ask that you keep me and my baby healthy as I carry this child. I know that I will do the best that I can, and that I can only trust in you.* Sharon drove up into Monica's driveway and went straight to her mailbox. It was full. She unlocked the door and went inside of the house. She placed the mail down on the table in the foyer before going in and checking the rest of the house. Once she was convinced that everything was okay, she locked up and walk cross the yard to Max's house to check and see how things were going with Diamond. She didn't get an answer when she rang the doorbell and knocked on the door, so she walked back cross the yard and got into her vehicle and drove off. Sharon headed straight towards the mall, she wanted to do some shopping for her, plus she needed to start getting some things for the baby.

Let me start in Motherland and see what I can get from out of here to wear, Sharon thought. Sharon started browsing around in the store looking for something nice and cute to wear. She pulled a top from a rack. *This blouse is pretty plus I can get it in three different colors. I will get each color with a pair of jeans that are popular with expecting moms,* she thought as she held the blouse up to her body and posed in front of the mirror. When Sharon left out of Motherland she had three bags in her hand. *Now I didn't intend to buy this much out of one store. I'm going to Babies-R-Us and get some stuff for this little one. Oh, I'm going to go crazy in here. I want to buy everything in here,* Sharon thought as she looked around the store. "I know if I had Monica with me she would have a fit buying stuff. I can just see her now," Sharon mumbled under her breath. Sharon walked around in the store for an hour and when she finally walked out of Babies-R-Us she had three more bags. *I've got to get to my car. This is just too many bags for me to carry. Once I put these bags in the trunk of my vehicle I can come back and shop some more,* she thought. While Sharon was walking to her car she started to feeling light headed, when she made it to her vehicle she put her bags in the car and sat down. *Why am I feeling this way? Oh my...I have not eaten since early this morning. This baby is hungry. I'm going to run to the food court and grab something real quick,* she thought as she got out of her vehicle. Sharon started towards the food court, by time she got to the counter to place her order, she fainted.

Darryl

As Darryl was getting out of his vehicle he proceeded to walk towards the mall entrance. He saw all of the commotion and was wondering what was going on. Once he got closer he saw a slight image of the woman's face. *It can't be. That can't be Sharon; she would not be hanging out at the mall at this time of the afternoon. This is usually her appointment time with her clients,* he thought as he moved through the crowd. When Darryl got up to the front by the food court he asked one of the patrons a question.

"What happened? Is everything all right with the lady?"

"I think she's going to be okay. All I know is that she was walking up this way and just about to place her order when she fainted. I do know that she is pregnant." Darryl moved through the crowd so that he could get a better look to satisfy his mind, but when he was able to see clearly enough he saw that it was Sharon. Immediate Darryl went to her side calling her name.

"Sharon! Sharon! Baby, can you hear me? Has anyone called the paramedics?" he asked, looking around at the crowd.

"Yes," a woman answered, "they are on their way."

Darryl stayed by Sharon's side until they got there. When the paramedics made it Darryl was asked to move so that they could tend to her. They started taking her blood pressure and listening to her heart. Then they put her on a stretcher and headed to the ambulance. Darryl was right on their heels. He was going to get in the back with the guy.

"Sir, do you know this woman?"

"Yes, I do, she's a friend of mine. I'm going to ride with you to the hospital."

"Why don't you take your car so that someone can bring her back, just in case she is release from the hospital?"

"Okay, I will." Darryl trailed the ambulance down the road speeding. All he could think about while driving was if Sharon and the baby were all right. He didn't know what he would do if something happened to them. He began to say a pray asking God to keep them both. At this moment he was so scared he just wanted them to be okay. Once the ambulance pulled into the emergency parking lot they rushed out with Sharon. Darryl pulled right behind them and jumped out of his car. Once inside the hospital, they took her straight to the back and started examining her. Darryl waited out in the waiting room nervous as a wreck. He needed to know what was going on with her so he went to the registration desk to ask if they knew anything yet.

"Ms., Could you tell me if the young lady that they just brought in is okay? I have been out here for a while now and no one has told me anything."

"Give me her name, please," the nurse said looking at her computer screen.

"Sharon Davis."

"Okay, I see here that the doctor is almost done with her. She will be going into a room shortly. They want to keep her overnight for observation just to make sure everything is okay. When the doctor comes out of the examination room I will direct him to you," she said with a reassuring smile.

"Thank you." Darryl walked down the hall to call his mother to let her know what happened, he would also have to call Sharon's father to let him know what was going on.

"Hey Mom."

"Hey baby, what's going on? Is everything okay? You're calling me back too soon."

"It's not good. I was calling to tell you that Sharon is in the hospital, she fainted at the mall. I'm here at the hospital with her now. The doctor hasn't come out of the exam room yet to let me know what happened. But I wanted to call and tell you."

"Darryl, I'm sorry. Do you need me to come up there?"

"No, mom, I don't want to alarm her anymore than she already is. She doesn't even know that I'm here. She was out of it when I got to her. But when I find out all the details I will call you back and let you know."

"Okay, baby. I'll be waiting, love you."

"Love you too mom." By the time Darryl finished talking with his mother the doctor was walking towards him.

"Hi, I'm Doctor Hector. I have been attending to Mrs. Davis," he said extending his hand to Darryl.

"How is she?" Darryl asked as he shook the doctor's hand.

"She is fine. She was a little dehydrated, plus she hadn't eaten anything all day. Her blood pressure is a little high that's why I want to keep her overnight to keep a watch on her. But other than that, everything else seems to be good. She will be going up to a room in a while, I have already ordered her a food tray, if you want you can go in and see her now."

"Thank you, doctor." Darryl went inside the examination room. Sharon was lying on her back looking at the television holding her stomach. You could tell that she had been crying because of her puffy red eyes. She was so into her own world that she didn't hear Darryl when he entered the room.

"Hello Sharon, how are you feeling? I know that you are surprised to see me."

"Yes, I am. Who called you? Why are you here Darryl?"

"I was walking into the mall when I saw the crowd of people. When I walked up and saw it was you I stayed by your side. I know I'm the last person you want to see, but I refuse to let you be here by yourself. I can call your father if you like."

"I already have. He's on his way."

"Look, Sharon, I know you don't want me here, but I'm this baby's father, I do have a right to be here. I plan on being in this child's life regardless of how you feel about me. This baby is all I have now. I know that you hate me now but if you would put your feelings of hate aside for a minute and think about how we can work things out for the baby, then that would be good. I know what I did was wrong, but I have been praying to God for forgiveness. I want a life with you and I'm going to do everything in my power to see to it that we have that. I can't see this child not having both parents."

"Darryl, I don't want to discuss this now, I just want to rest so that I can go home tomorrow."

"Okay, okay, but what about your car, how do you plan on getting it?"

"I can't worry about that right now."

"I can take your father back there so that he can take it to your house."

"I guess that would be good. So tell me, what where you doing at the mall? Picking up new women?"

"That was a low blow."

"Not as low as it's going to get," Sharon replied with an attitude.

"Come on Sharon, let's stop with the comments. You want to know what I was doing at the mall, right? So let me tell you. I needed to get away from the office so that I could clear my mind. I don't want to talk about it while you are like this, but I can tell you that we are about to begin our divorce process. What were you doing out there? You usually have clients around that time."

"I had just left the doctor's office for my appointment, then I drove over to Monica's house to check on things because she is out of town. I thought I would treat myself to some maternity clothes and look for the baby some stuff. I started feeling bad when I was walking to the car, then I realized that I hadn't eaten anything. I decided to go back and get something from the food court and that's the last thing I remember."

"I'm glad it was nothing worse than that. Sharon I miss you. I think about you all the time—the things we use to do, how we use to make each other laugh. Could you find it in your heart to forgive me? I'm sorry, you just said that it wasn't the time for this and you're right. But you have to know that I never meant to hurt you, please understand it. I don't care about anything right now, but you and the baby, and if it takes every minute, every second, I don't care how long—I'm not giving up on you." By the time Darryl finished talking to Sharon her father walked into the room.

Monica/Desire'

"Well, hello Monica, don't you look beautiful. The color of that blouse brings out the color in your eyes. I knew from the first time I saw you on the cover of the magazine that you were more beautiful in person."

"Thank you, you're looking mighty handsome yourself. I just want you to know that this is not something that I do all of the time. I really don't know why I agreed to this date, after you told me you were the boss."

"Well, I can tell you this, you won't regret this evening. I'm going to show you a good time and don't even think about work tomorrow because everyone already knows that they have the day off."

Monica laughed. "It must be great being the boss." They both started laughing as they were walking out of the door. Monica's mouth fell open when she saw what Desire' had waiting for them once they reach the front doors of the lobby. He had a horse and carriage waiting on them, one black horse and one white horse. They stood so tall and pretty. The driver was wearing a black tuxedo and holding a bouquet of flowers. As they walked toward the carriage, Monica whispered to Desire', "This is nice."

"I told you that you are about to have a wonderful night. I wanted to do something different from other dates that you have been on so that you will go out with me again." As they rode around the city looking at all of the beautiful buildings they made small talk. "I figured if I pulled out all stops on this date, then maybe you'll consider going out with me again before you leave."

"And what about your girlfriend? Will she be happy with you taking me out? A man of your status is bound to have a woman stashed away somewhere," Monica said while waving her hand through the air.

"No I don't. My last relationship ended six months ago."

"Sorry, I didn't mean to bring up bad feelings."

"It's okay, I've gotten over it. I can say at first it was difficult for me because I was truly in love with her. She didn't have to want for anything. But my job requires high demands. She was told this from the beginning. I asked her could she deal with my lifestyle and she said yes, but I guess things became too much for her and she wanted out. The good thing is that we departed on good terms. We knew that it was hard for each other and we tried to deal with it, but it just wasn't meant to be."

"And you guys have been apart for six months?"

"Yeah, I see her every now and then. She found someone who can give her that quality time that she deserves. She's engaged to be married, and the wedding is taking place pretty soon." Before Desire' could finish his sentence they were pulling up at the restaurant. "This place right here is another one of my favorites. You are going to love the food here, I try to make it here at least once a week."

"Okay, well I'm going to see if it beats where GI-GI and I ate the other night." Desire' extended his hand and assisted Monica out of the carriage. She left her flowers in the carriage. Desire' paid the driver for bringing them to their destination, and gave him a generous tip. As they walked into the restaurant hand-in-hand, Monica felt so special. She hadn't been on a date in a while and she was really feeling the attention. Once inside the restaurant they were lead to the back where the music was playing softly by a band, the lights were low and as she looked around she saw that they were the only two in there.

"Are they about to close or what? We are the only people here," Monica replied in astonishment.

"No, they are not, I rented this part out for us only. I do not want to be disturbed by anyone but the people who are serving us." Desire' had this look on his face that made him look like a little boy, but it was a cute look. Desire' pulled the chair out for her and once she was seated, he seated himself. The flickering light from the candle on the table illuminated their faces with a soft glow. It was so romantic Monica's panties were getting wet just thinking about how he would look naked lying next to her.

"This is really nice. I can honestly say that I'm really enjoying myself so far. So tell me a little about yourself, you don't have to give it all to me tonight."

"So are you saying that I will get another date with you before you return back home?"

"You might." They both started laughing. By this time the waiter was coming over to take their order.

"Bonsoir madame and monsieur."

"Bonsoir, but we will be speaking English tonight."

"Okay, so what will you be having tonight? Would you like to start off with a nice wine until you decide?"

"That would be great, let me order a bottle of your Le vin blanc. This is a white wine, it's very good. It is smooth and has a light taste to it, one of their best to me. Like I say, this is one of my favorites. So what would you like for dinner?"

"I'm going to let you choose for me. I want to see if you have what it takes when it comes to food. Since you said that it was one of your favorite places and you have rented out this side for us, then you will take control tonight."

Desire' had a look on his face like 'Oh, for real, *everything?'*

"Umm, maybe I'm going to have to take that back, because there's just something about that look on your face that might get me in trouble." Desire' started smiling then. "So back to my question: tell me about you."

"Well, I'm the oldest of five, I have two sister, and two brothers. All of us are in the business together. Yes, I am the owner of my clothing line, but my sister's help run it. My brothers and I have our own restaurant here, but they do most of the work because I'm so busy with the clothing business. They all have other jobs on the side, but we all work these two together. Both of my parents are still living, they are retired. Both of my sister's are married, one to a doctor, and the other to a contractor. One of my brothers is single and one is married to a teacher. We are a close family. We always get together and have a family night at our parent's house once a month. I really do love my family, I would go through hell and hot water for them and I know that they would do the same for me.

Monica was so amazed as she listened to him, she wanted the same thing with her mother. Her mother and her brother were close but somewhere down the line her relationship with her mother changed. But she was going to make it her business to visit her mom when she got back home.

"I will have to let you meet them before you leave, if that's okay with you."

"Sure." By this time the waiter was coming back with their wine. He poured the wine in their glasses. Monica lifted hers, and Desire' motioned with his hand for her to wait.

"Let me taste it first to make sure it's okay." Desire' took a sip of the wine and agreed that it was good. Everything is fine with it, thank you," he said to the waiter.

"Are you ready to order now? If not, I can come back later," the waiter replied.

"No, we are ready. I would like to order the Pot Au feu with a Baguette, also could we have a salad and for dessert we would like the Choux a' la Cream. That will be all."

"I'll return with your food shortly."

Monica was looking at Desire' wondering what in the word did he just order, but the way that the words rolled off of his lips made him sound so sexy, she couldn't wait to tell Sharon about this date.

"So Desire', what was it that you just order for us?"

"Oh, you don't trust me? Remember you just said that I'm in control, and you were going to let me handle this. I'll tell you after you eat it, once you see how goooood it's going to be," he said with a wink. "So, how is the wine? If it's not to your liking I can always order another bottle."

"No, it's good. I just hope it doesn't get me like the last bottle of wine I had the other night," she laughed. "Desire', you are a very interesting man and I'm wondering how you just happened to come upon our name."

"Well, I can tell you this, I had been searching all over the States for a new face to model my new line and I came upon your face and was captivated by your beauty. Really, my brother brought you to my attention. He brought a magazine of you to me one day and I knew from that day that I had to meet you. I would look at your picture every day and wonder how I could get you. One day I had my people look you up. I told them to find out who you were and get you here ASAP. I know that it might sound funny, but you are *special* to me and this is my first date with you. There's just something about you that captivates me, and I intend to find out all about you."

Monica was speechless. She just sat there amazed by what she had just heard. This was not what she expected to hear. So she took a drink of her wine and just nodded her head. "I don't know what to say."

"Don't say anything, just let me show you what it could be like with us. I want to spend as much time with you as I can while you are here. I want to learn all about you and for you to learn all about me. If you just give me that much you will see that we do belong together." Their food arrived at their table. They began to eat and make conversation. Everything was perfect; the music that played along as they ate made the mood so romantic. Once they were finished with dinner and desserts,

Desire' paid the ticket and gave the waiter a generous tip. He pulled Monica's chair out so that she could stand and they headed toward the front door. When they walked out front Monica looked confused. She didn't see the carriage.

"Desire', what happened to the carriage? He was supposed to stay until we finished with dinner, plus he has my flowers. Maybe we need to go back in until he arrives?"

"No, we don't have to go back inside. Our ride is right in front of us. See, that was our carriage here, now we will have a limo ride to our destination. See baby, I told you I'm going to show you how your date is suppose to be." Monica's face lit up with a smile. Desire' and Monica walked hand-in-hand towards the limo. Once they reach it the driver opened the door and helped them in. In the back was a television, a small bar, her flowers and a card with her name on it.

"What is this Desire'? You are really going overboard here."

"No, I'm not. This is our special night and I want it to be a night for you to remember. When you close your eyes at night, all I want you to see is us. So open the card and read it." Monica did just that and when she finished she found herself wrapping her arms around his neck and giving him a kiss on the lips. This took Desire' totally by surprise. He knew then that he was on the right road with her and he had to stay that way if he wanted to marry her. Monica didn't know this, but he had his heart set on the two of them getting married. He'd known this from the moment he laid eyes on her picture.

"Thank you! Those were beautiful words, very well-written. I will cherish this card forever. No one has ever expressed words to me like this."

"Well, sit back and enjoy the ride because it's going to take us about forty-five minutes before we get to where we are going." Monica laid her head back and thought about how the night had been great so far and that she was really having a good time.

"You know Desire', you told me a little about your family so I guess I can tell you a little something about me. I grew up in Atlanta, Georgia and moved when I went off to school. My mom and I were close when I was growing up, but when I got in high school things changed between us for some reason. I think it was the fact that she just didn't have time for me anymore. All she wanted to do was party every weekend which allowed me to be free. If it wasn't for my best friend Sharon I probably would have had a baby right now or been on drugs somewhere. When I get back home I'm planning on going to see her, she is sick now with cancer and not doing too good at all."

" Are you the only child?"

"No. I have a brother that is still in Atlanta. He's a lawyer. He takes excellent care of her. She's not in a nursing home, she lives with him. He has someone to come and care for her while he is at work. I do send money once a month to help out, though. I know it's not a lot, but it's just every time I go home to see her we end up fussing about something. I had already told myself once I returned home I'm going to make things right with me and my mom."

"I can't say how I'd feel if my mother and I were in a situation like that, but I do know that I would do what you just said. I would go and make things right. You never know what tomorrow brings." By this time they were pulling up at the cottage. "This is our last stop. This is one of my favorite places to visit when I'm feeling down about something. I'm able to think with a clear mind and make the right choices. I wanted to bring you here so that you can see how nature really makes you feel free. Come on let's get out so you can see the inside." They exited the limo and walked up towards the cottage. Once Desire' opened the door the setting was beautiful. There were candles everywhere, soft music was playing and there was wine with an assortment of different cheeses on the table; along with rose petals everywhere. Also, there was a box that sat on the table with Monica's name printed across it. Desire' had it special made for her by a designer called "WINK.

"This is so BEAUTIFUL! I can say I have never had a night like this one. Thank you, thank you for everything! I'm glad I decided to come on this date. You have really made me feel special. I was scared to go out with you, but Sharon told me to go on and have fun, and I have had one of the best nights ever." Monica walked around just loving every moment of this. She did not want to miss anything; she wanted to keep this image of this fabulous night in her head. She went to the window and just stood gazing out of the window smiling at how wonderful this trip had turned out to be.

"Hey Monica, this is for you." She turned around and saw that Desire had the box with her name written across it. He handed it to her. "This is for you," he repeated again. "When I saw it I only thought of you, knowing how gorgeous it would look on you."

"Desire', you shouldn't have. You have given me so much tonight I can't take this from you."

"Yes, you can, and you will. This is just the beginning. So here, open this box and I hope you like what's in here." Monica opened the box and to her surprise it was a beautiful bracelet. Hanging from the chain was a clear glass heart with her initial M. engraved on it. Her mouth just dropped open. When Desire' put it on her arm it fit perfectly. "Oh my God this is gorgeous, I love it. I will not take this off, ever."

"I was hoping that you would love it and that you would say that. I had this made especially for you by a good friend of mine. She is founder and designer of "WINK" Jewel. This is the only person that I have ever purchased jewelry from for my mother, and sisters, now you. Come over here let me get you a glass of wine, we can grab a bite of cheese, sit on the blanket by candlelight and just talk."

"What about the driver, is he going to be out there until we get ready to leave?"

"No, he's gone. We won't be leaving here until morning. There are two bedrooms here, you don't have to worry about anything to sleep in. I already know your size so you have some night clothes and anything else that you might need already here. Don't worry, I'm not going to hurt you in any kind of way and I will never let anyone else hurt you. You are so beautiful and whether you know it or not, I'm going to make you my wife. I knew I had to have you, that's why I went through everything necessary to get you here."

For some reason Monica didn't fear this man, she just wanted to be in his arms right now. So she placed her head on his chest and closed her eyes. "Would you make love to me tonight?" she asked, looking him straight in the eyes.

"Yes, if that's what you want."

"I do." They began to kiss passionately wrapped in each other's arms on the floor. It was so heated. Desire' slowly took off Monica's clothes while she took his off. They stood naked looking at each other amazed how both of their bodies were perfect. Desire' lead Monica upstairs to the large bedroom where there was a king size bed, lounge chair, a flat screen television, a bathroom with a huge shower, and a huge fireplace. The roaring fire made the room feel warm and cozy. It was so romantic. Desire' laid Monica on the bed and his eyes drank in every inch of her beautiful body. He just wanted to capture this imagine of her and keep it in his heart.

"Are you sure, you want to do this? Because we don't have to."

"I'm ready. I know what I want and that is you, I'm feeling this and this moment is perfect." After Monica spoke those words Desire' kissed her body from head to toe. He sucked on each of her toes one at a time, she was so mesmerized by this that she could not hold back the noise that was coming from her mouth. Desire' kissed and licked his way back up toward her body. Then he began to kiss her wet vagina. Monica was sooo wet, but she did not want to cum just yet. She wanted to explode with him inside of her. Desire' ate her pussy so good that she wanted him to put his dick inside of her right then. But he would not.

"Desire', I need you inside of me. I'm about to cum," she whispered.

"I'm sorry, but I cannot. I haven't even sucked your breast yet."

"I don't think I can take anymore, I'm just about at the edge. I need you inside of me, this feels so good. You have wet my whole body with your tongue."

"Turn over," he instructed. Monica turned over like she was asked and Desire' started on her back. He kissed every inch of her back down to her butt. Monica was about to crawl out of bed because it was feeling so good, she grabbed the pillow holding it tightly as Desire' ate her from the back.

"Desire', you have to stop please, if you don't I'm going to cum." At that moment Desire' took his nine inch dick and entered Monica's pussy from the back. He made love to her so gently that she took the pain from his huge dick along with the pleasure. They made love over an hour before they both exploded together. Once they were finished Monica laid her head on Desire's chest and told him all about her and he did the same before they drifted off to sleep.

Tameka

Once Tameka left Darryl's office she felt a sense of relief. It was like a load had been lifted off of her. She smiled as she walked to her vehicle and thought to herself that she would go to the mall and treat herself to something. She said to herself, "This Too Shall Pass." Yes, it still hurts but I'm going to be all right as long as I got God with me. Tameka drove down Highway 150 and listened to her music. She knew that she wanted to go to the linen department when she got to the mall, because she wanted to change everything in her bedroom. She wanted to remove the memories of Darryl out of her life completely. Once Tameka reached the parking lot of the mall she could not decide where she wanted to start. Once she got inside all she knew was that it was time to look out for her.

I think I'll go inside of Belk's and see what they have first and afterwards I'll check out Linen's and Things, she thought. She took a final look at herself in the mirror and once she saw that she was perfect, she opened the door, got out, and headed towards the mall. Tameka was caught up in her thoughts...*This is a perfect day to be out. I'm going to make this day and every other day all about me.*

God, I thank You for giving me the courage to do what I did today, because if it hadn't been for you, I would have "SNAPPED ON DARRYL." Tameka walked inside of Belk's and went right to the linen department. She knew what color she had in mind she was just hoping that they would have that color. "Everything is so pretty I don't know what to choose from. Those lamps over there are just what I want. That leopard print, let me get those," she spoke out loud to no one in particular. And when she walked closer to get the lamps she saw some pillows too. When Tameka left out of Belk's she had purchased over $400 worth of merchandise.

As Tameka was walking towards the entrance to put the items in the trunk of her vehicle she spotted a bathroom set that would match the bedroom. *I want all memories gone from that house. I know that right now I can't erase the memories in my head and heart, but as each day passes they will also pass too. Let me get this stuff out of the way and I will be back to get that,* she thought. Tameka reached her truck and put all of her items in the back. She was headed back into the mall to see what else she wanted to get but before she could reach to open the door, a strong hand opened the door for her. She looked up and saw the most attractive man ever. "Thank you!" she said to him with a smile.

"It's my pleasure."

As she began walking through the mall she could not keep her mind off of the gentleman who had opened the door for her. She could still smell the scent of his cologne, and she liked it. While Tameka walked around the mall for a while she did not see anything else that she wanted at that moment, so she decided to go and get her something to eat. While she stood at the hot dog counter to place her order, she heard a voice behind her. "So I see you again?" he asked.

This time she could not help herself, she responded back to him. "Yes, you do. Are you following me or something?"

"No, I was also hungry for a hot dog and I'm glad that I was because I get to see you again."

"You are full of it."

"If you say so, but may I have the pleasure of asking you your name?"

"Tameka, and yours?"

"Phillip," he said extending his hand.

"Nice to meet you Phillip," Tameka replied shaking his hand. He didn't appear to want to let it go.

"Same here Tameka, so are you going to eat here, or are you leaving? I would love to share this moment with you, you know, eating on hot dogs." He flashed another smile.

"Well, I'm kind of in a hurry."

"Oh, come on. It's only hot dogs and a conversation."

Tameka took a moment to think about it before she decided to eat with him. "Okay, I'll eat my hot dogs with you."

The two sat down at the table near the corner. They shared small talk, hot dogs and drinks.

Shelia/Marcus

Once the pizza arrived Shelia and Marcus ate while they watched a movie. They were both into the movie, it was one of her favorites and Marcus happened to just have it *New Jack City*. She'd always thought that Wesley Snipes was sexy to her and could watch it over and over.

"Would you like me to pour you another glass of wine?"

"Sure, I can use another one after tonight. You know Marcus, I know that we were supposed to be somewhere else tonight..."

"Listen, don't worry about that as long as you are here safe and that fool is in jail. I'm just glad that the cops saw everything. There's no telling what he may have done. So stop with the apologizing, we are still on our date, we are at my place and we are together. That's all that matters to me."

After Marcus explained that to Shelia he leaned over and gave her a sweet kiss on her lips, then he moved down to her neck, her shoulders, and her breast. Marcus began to take off her clothes. He wanted to kiss every part of her body. He wanted to take control of her making her shiver all over as he took every inch of her in. By the time Marcus finished bathing Shelia with his tongue the movie had gone off and she was now on the floor with her legs spread wide open. The only sounds coming from her mouth were the sounds of moaning. Shelia had cum at least twice and she wanted to make Marcus feel good too. So between her moans she told Marcus to turn over so that she could give him the pleasure that he needed. Marcus turned over and Shelia took his nine inch dick into her mouth and gave him the best head job that he ever had. She then took her finger and stuck it in his ass and maneuvered it around as she sucked on his dick. Marcus shot cum all in Shelia's mouth and she swallowed it all down. Once they finished the erotic lovemaking they both laid on the floor looking off into the darkness as their eyes got heavy and they feel asleep.

Henry/Sharon

When the door to the hospital room opened causing some light to come into the room, Sharon looked up from Darryl and saw that it was her dad. She smiled and tears formed in her eyes because she knew then that the most important person in her life at that moment had come to her side.

"Dad!"

"Baby girl, how are you? I came as fast as I could. You had me scared half to death. Your mom's already gone, what would I do without my special girl?"

"I'm sorry, I didn't mean to get you all upset. I'm just glad that you are here that's what important to me."

"Tell me what happened?"

"I was at the mall doing some shopping after I left Monica's house checking her mail. I had already been in the mall and I was at my car putting my bags in it. Then I realized that I hadn't eaten all day. By the time I headed back to get something, I fainted. I don't remember much after that. But I ended up here."

"What did the doctor say?"

By this time Darryl stood up to introduce himself because Sharon had not acknowledged him yet. And since all of Mr. Davis's attention was focused on his daughter he didn't even see Darryl sitting in the chair. When Darryl stood up the sound of the chair got Mr. Davis's attention and that's what made him notice that someone else was in the room.

"Hi Mr. Davis, I'm Darryl."

"Hi Darryl, I'm Henry, Sharon's father. I know from listening to your conversation."

"Are you a friend of my daughters?"

"As a matter of fact, I am sir. I'm the baby's father." The look on Mr. Davis's face told Darryl that her father knew the story about them.

"Well Darryl, it's nice to finally meet the man who has my daughter with child. Have you heard anything from the doctor about my daughter?"

Yes sir, I have, they are planning on keeping her overnight just for observation. She was dehydrated and her blood pressure was high, they want to keep a watch on it. He also told me that he has ordered her some food so that she could eat something."

"So you haven't seen the doctor yet, baby girl?"

"No." By that time the doctor was walking into the room with a young lady behind him with a food tray. He introduced himself and gave everyone the update on what was going on with Sharon. Everyone was relieved that she was going to be okay and that the baby was okay, but they were going to do an ultrasound on her in the morning before she left the hospital to make sure that she was fine.

After the doctor left the room Mr. Davis told Darryl that he would be staying at the hospital with Sharon and if he needed to leave he could. She would be okay. Darryl left, but he let Sharon know that he would be back in the morning to see her. Sharon didn't want to get into a fussing match with Darryl so she told him okay.

The next morning when Darryl walked into Sharon's room she was not there, neither was Mr. Davis. He wondered did they already leave the hospital so he went to the reception desk to see if Sharon had been discharged. By the time he got to the desk someone called his name. Darryl turned around to see who it was.

"I was just about to see if she had checked out. I went to the room and no one was in there."

"Yeah, I know, I went to get some breakfast while they took her to get the ultrasound. They said she should be back in about forty-five minutes depending on how many are ahead of her."

"Okay, so how are you doing this morning, Mr. Davis?"

"I'm good, knowing that my baby girl is going to be all right."

"I know, I just don't know what I would do if anything happen to her and the baby. I know that she has told you everything and I know you don't care for me in particular, but out of all that has happened I do want you to know that I love that girl, and I'm not going to let her raise that baby alone. I will be a part of the baby's life."

"Listen son, I have told my daughter to let you be a part of the baby's life, I am not the one to judge you or her, but I will not allow you to hurt my daughter a second time. Right now she is very embarrassed about this, but I have told her to keep her head up and go on with her life. Everyone makes mistakes, but we know not to fall back into that boat again. I don't know you that well, but I do sense that you really care about my daughter. You are going to have to give her time to digest all of this and let her make her decision about your relationship." Darryl and Mr. Davis continued in deep conversation, that's when Sharon arrived back to the room. They hadn't noticed that she had come back until she called out to her dad.

"Dad! Dad!" she called as they wheeled her into the room.

"Hey baby girl, are you about ready?"

"Yes, they said that everything is good and for me to see my doctor in three days."

"Okay, so are you ready to check out of here?"

"I sure am. I want to be in my own bed."

"Okay, let's get your things and go."

"Where's my car?"

"It's still at the mall."

"I told you Sharon that your father and I can get your car home to you."

"We sure can, once we get you settled in we will go and get your car."

"That's fine."

When patient escort came to the room with Sharon's wheelchair they all left the room walking down the aisle of the hospital. Once Sharon got into her father car and Darryl in his truck, they pulled out headed towards Sharon's house.

About the Author

Kandise Carlisle was born and raised in Birmingham, Alabama. She continues to live there with her two beautiful daughters. She has a love for writing, reading, and praise dancing. Her passion for writing started when she was in elementary school when she would write plays for the class. She would often ask God to show her what He wanted her to write. When writing, her imagination takes her to another world; a world where she lives out her experiences on paper. She currently works at Quest Diagnostics and is currently working on Part 2 of "Open Heart with Closed Eyes."

Interested in joining our Pink Kiss Publishing family? Visit our website for more details!
www.pinkkisspublishing.com

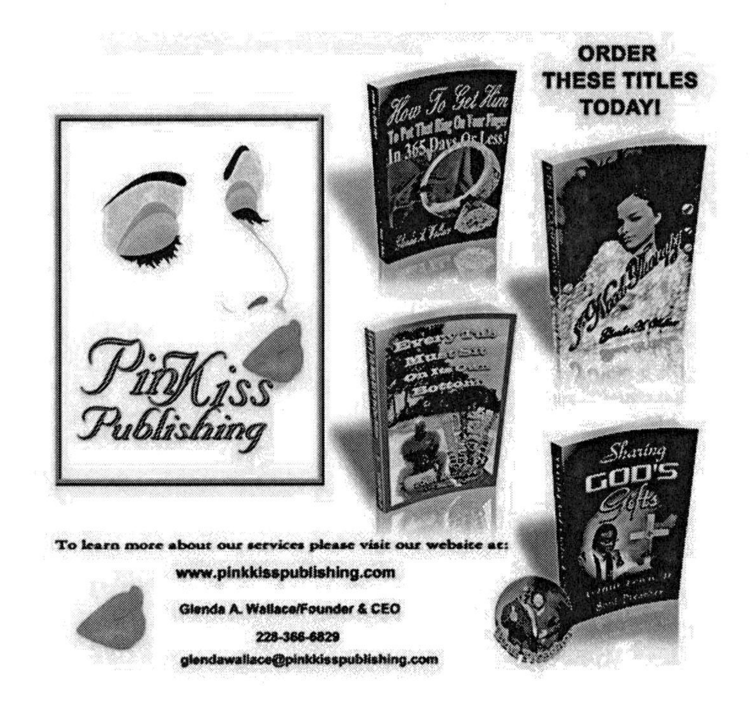

Pink Kiss Publishing Company
Attn: Glenda A. Wallace
P.O. Box 744
Gautier, MS 39553
228-366-6829 / Office
228-205-3610 / Fax
glendawallace@pinkkisspublishing.com

CPSIA information can be obtained
at www.ICGtesting.com
Printed in the USA
FFOW01n1332111113
2336FF